NERO: SHATTERED WINGS

RUSSIAN MOB CHRONICLES
BOOK 6

SHANDI BOYES

COPYRIGHT

Written By: Shandi Boyes

Editing: Courtney Umpires

Cover: SSB Covers and Designs

Photography: Wander Aguiar

Proofreading: Lindsi La Bar

ALSO BY SHANDI BOYES

Denotes Standalone Books

Perception Series

Saving Noah *

Fighting Jacob *

Taming Nick *

Redeeming Slater *

Saving Emily

Wrapped Up with Rise Up

Protecting Nicole *

Enigma Series

Enigma

Unraveling an Enigma

Enigma The Mystery Unmasked

Enigma: The Final Chapter

Beneath The Secrets

Beneath The Sheets

Spy Thy Neighbor *

The Opposite Effect *

I Married a Mob Boss *

Second Shot *

The Way We Are

The Way We Were

Sugar and Spice *

Lady In Waiting

Man in Queue

Couple on Hold

Enigma: The Wedding

Silent Vigilante

Hushed Guardian

Quiet Protector

Enigma: An Isaac Retelling

Twisted Lies *

Bound Series

Chains

Links

Bound

Restrain

The Misfits *

Nanny Dispute *

Russian Mob Chronicles

Nikolai: Resurrecting the Bratva

Nikolai: Resurrecting the Bratva

Nikolai: Ruling the Bratva

Asher: My Russian Revenge *

Trey *

Nero: Shattered Wings *

The Italian Cartel

Dimitri

Roxanne

Reign

Mafia Ties (Novella)

Maddox

Demi

Ox

Rocco *

Clover *

Smith *

RomCom Standalones

Just Playin' *

Ain't Happenin' *

The Drop Zone *

Very Unlikely *

False Start *

Short Stories - Newsletter Downloads

Christmas Trio *

Falling For A Stranger *

One Night Only Series

Hotshot Boss *

Hotshot Neighbor *

The Bobrov Bratva Series

Wicked Intentions *

Sinful Intentions *

Devious Intentions *

Deadly Intentions *

Martial Privilege Series

Doctored Vows *

Deceitful Vows *

Vengeful Vows *

Broken Vows *

BLURB

Minutes after being served divorce papers, I receive a phone call that warps my mind.

If it isn't bad enough my soon-to-be ex filed for divorce on our fourteenth wedding anniversary, he also used my company card to spoil his mistress with a honeymoon suite and a thousand dollar floral arrangement.

I've not been handed a single flower since the day we wed, so when the hotel clerk requests to see my card before processing the payment, I accept the opportunity unknowingly granted to me.

With the tiny teddy I had hoped would milk my husband of one measly orgasm covered by a thin coat, and my cell phone recording, I burst into the honeymoon suite, gung-ho for the evidence that will offer me the ultimate revenge.

There isn't a single person in the entire suite.

A god, though. There's one of them.

He glares at me like I was the one caught cheating, and the heat of his stare makes me wish that were true.

I'd sign on the dotted line without protest just for the chance of spending an hour with the dark and brooding stranger who doesn't look at me like I should cover my curves with an outfit "more appropriate for my body type."

Nero loves the way I fill in the racy little number, and he's more than happy to spend a few hours ensuring my husband knows exactly what he let go, and to help me repair my shattered wings.

*

Nero is a standalone bratva (Russian Mafia) romance about two people who wanted revenge, but instead, found each other.

WANT TO STAY IN TOUCH?

Facebook: facebook.com/authorshandi

Instagram: instagram.com/authorshandi

Email: authorshandi@gmail.com

Reader's Group: bit.ly/ShandiBookBabes

Website: authorshandi.com

Newsletter: https://www.subscribepage.com/AuthorShandi

1

MIRANDA

*W*hen I look in the mirror, I grimace when I see how the crisscross pattern of my teddy clings to my body.

The changing-room mirrors at the boutique store I popped into last month must be those flattering, you'll-never-look-fat-in-our-store mirrors, because this ensemble looks nothing like the one I tried on weeks ago.

I'm meant to be spicing up my marriage, not giving Roy more reasons to whine.

This hot little number is supposed to complement my curves. It's made them offensive.

Roy will complain that there's too much skin showing. He's such an ass he'll probably say I look like a pork roll held together by a mesh cooking bag.

As much as this kills me to admit, his hurtful comments aren't far from the truth. My tummy has more cellulite than a man seeking a trophy wife would find acceptable.

Furthermore, due to a hectic pre-Christmas work schedule, my thighs are chunky enough that they clap when I walk.

While getting ready, I scared my Jack Russell terrier, Tempy, more than the luminous clouds darkening my hometown's sky hours earlier than usual did. She's a chicken when it comes to storms. Her tummy has been a bundle of nerves all evening.

Mine hasn't been much better. Although I've been married for fourteen years, my stomach still gets butterflies whenever I dress up for a special occasion.

They're not good flutters.

I can't recall the last time Roy and I had sex. I think it was Easter the previous year...

Actually, scrap that. His aunt had an emergency not long after we exchanged sugar-laden gifts. I ate his share of our treats *and* mine.

My stomach hurt for days, and the scale was just as damning the following week, but it was the most satisfied I've *ever* been.

My plump lips arch at one side when I twirl, taking in the entire package.

Not bad, Miranda. Not bad at all.

I have plenty of junk in the trunk to deviate even the most disinterested man's eyes from my stomach, and a trip to the salon this afternoon did wonders for my hair.

My face isn't half bad, either.

As my grandma always said, a couple of pounds on the scale will plump out any pesky wrinkles.

I appear closer to mid-twenties than mid-thirties and look put together. Possibly hot.

I doubt my husband will agree, though. He hasn't issued a single compliment since we exchanged vows.

Ugh! Why do I put myself through the torment?

Roy is a dick. I should have left him years ago. It is just hard to remember a life without him in it. He swept me off my feet when I was young and dumb and when he could cover his flaws with a rigidly sharp jaw and a handsome face that concealed all his lies.

I married him too fast. We hadn't even dated for six months.

It was fun at the start, but now that the shine has long worn off, I'm on the cusp of depression.

That's what my outfit is about. It's our anniversary, and as much as I wish I were in sweats, eating ice cream out of the tub and watching my favorite shows, I need to do something to re-spark our connection.

Roy promised our rut would only be temporary, so I must give him the chance to make true on his promise.

It is the most I can do since he's not kept a single one in the past fourteen years.

I flop onto my bed, sending sprigs of curly brown hair bouncing against the sheets I wrangled into submission only thirty minutes ago. I've changed the sheets, cooked a feast fit for a king, and rid my body of almost every hair it owns.

It's fortunate this week has been good, or I may have had a Britney Spears 2007 moment.

During the first bounce of the mattress springs, the doorbell rings. For a moment, I'm confused. Why would Roy need to knock? Then I remember how he lost his keys three months ago.

He was attending a business meeting almost an hour from here. He refused to call an Uber, so I had to drive over two hours to pick him up since I was at work.

Then I had to listen to him whine for another four hours while I finished my shift with the catering company I fought to get off the ground weeks shy of my twenty-first birthday.

We were short a staff member. Roy could have helped, but that seems to be beyond his capabilities. I'm unsure if he knows the definition of hard work. He's never touched a dustpan or dishcloth in his life.

All the chores are on my shoulders—including the "man" jobs like mowing, weeding, and edging.

"Just a minute," I shout when the doorbell buzzes again.

I race through the foyer of my modest yet cozy home, dodging Tempy and her excited twirls.

The floorplan of my home is a retro '70s layout but with the modern features you'd seek from a loft in New York. I love my home.

It and my catering business have been my only saving grace for the past decade.

After snagging a coat from a rack by the door, my intuition warning me that answering my caller's knocks in a mesh-and-rope teddy will only end one way—badly—I plaster a fake smile onto my face and pull open the door.

"Happy anniversary..."

My high-pitched celebratory tone croaks at the end, startled by the person at the door. It isn't Roy or Mrs. Gessler who often comes over for a cup of sugar and three hours of nonstop gossip.

It is a man with one leg longer than the other, a wonky smile, and slicked-back hair.

"Mrs. Martin?"

"Yes. Hello." I sound confused. Justly so. My name isn't on the deed of this house. Roy said not a single broker would take a risk on me since I was without stable employment.

He made it seem that my business has been in the red longer than its inaugural year and that his income outranks mine twenty to one.

For future reference, that isn't close to the truth.

My company is keeping on the gas, electricity, and every other silly gimmick Roy is adamant he can't live without. It has also paid the mortgage every month for the past six years.

"Are you seeking Roy?"

He seems like the type who'd work with Roy. His smile is cocky, but his composure screams that there's a stick shoved up his ass. It is as obvious as the alarm bells that rang in my head precisely fourteen years ago today.

When my caller's eyes remain steadfast on my chest, I tug my coat in tighter, mindful from the cool winds whipping through the door that my outfit offers little coverage.

"He should be back at any moment." Against the better judgment of my head, I open the door all the way and gesture for him to enter. "You can wait in the foyer."

He shakes his head, sending blond locks spilling down his face. "That's fine. I'm not here for Roy." He coughs before finally lifting his head. "I'm here for you."

"Me?" I touch my chest, returning his focus to my puckered

nipples barely concealed by a thin coat. It is chilly today. But I'm suddenly fretful it has nothing to do with the cool change the weather forecaster projected for the rest of the month.

My caller doesn't look up while saying, "I'm here to serve you these."

He thrusts an official-looking envelope my way. His grunt of disappointment when it covers my breasts ruffles the curls I left down to frame my heart-shaped face.

After another lingering stare, he sighs dramatically and then turns on his heel and leaves.

He barely makes it halfway down the footpath that will never require salting before he twists back around. A million words run through his head; however, he only speaks six. "Once you're sorted, look me up." I'm about to tell him I have no clue who he is, much less how to contact him, when he nudges his head to the envelope. "All my details are in there."

With a wink, he slips into the back of an idling town car and vanishes down the tree-lined street.

I stare in the direction he left for several seconds before lowering my eyes to the puffed-out envelope. The seal states it is from a law firm. It isn't the same firm Roy works for, but it is in the same zip code and specializes in the same field of expertise—divorce litigation.

As a cussword bounces off the walls of my home, I tear open the envelope and rip out the contents inside. It doesn't take a genius to work out what document I've been served. It is a petition for divorce, which was signed by Roy only an hour ago.

"You son of a bitch," I mutter when I read through the extensively noted document. He's not just seeking half of the assets we accumulated in our marriage. He wants the lot—including Tempy.

Tempy growls and barks, matching my sentiment to a T, as I continue perusing the document.

The attached proposed property settlement agitates my last nerve.

"Since Spouse One has recorded no payments toward the dwelling cited in I.II.A of the proposed settlement, Spouse Two gives three weeks' notice for the relocation of Spouse One."

It's three weeks until Christmas. Where exactly is he expecting me to go? All the hotels are booked out, and Roy ensured I cut all ties with my family within the first year of our marriage.

"Just a minute," I murmur for the second time this evening when Tempy barks again.

I appreciate her efforts to subdue my panic, but I don't think well when bombarded with multiple issues. I'm the worst multi-tasker. It isn't my fault. I learned from a master that effort is not a requirement for *anything*.

Roy never flicked my clit while driving into me. He barely cupped my breasts that jerked around as much as his jackrabbit hip thrusts. Multi isn't a part of *any* of his sexual conquests, and I've only ever been with him.

When Tempy barks again, the cause of her excitement is announced.

My cell phone is ringing.

I silenced it during my last event, not wanting the bride and groom angry about it blowing up every hour on the hour as it usually does when I attend functions known for love and promiscuity.

I live in Vegas. Lust and love go hand in hand, and the attention I got from single suitors in attendance once made Roy jealous as fuck.

His lack of contact today should have raised alarms long before I was served with divorce papers.

With my phone flashing a local area code, I snatch it up and slide my finger across the screen. I can't let any jobs go astray if I want to contest Roy's claim that I've not contributed a single dime to our home. I've paid the mortgage on time every month for years.

This home is more mine than his.

"Hello?"

A quick swallow commences a slow, unsure question. "Mrs. Martin?"

Her salutation smashes my back molars together. I hide my annoyance well. "Yes. How can I help you?"

"I'm sorry to bother you. I know it is your anniversary." She sounds young, less mature than the years I wasted married to Roy. "But I'm having some issues with the credit card you supplied."

"The card *I* supplied?"

Don't judge the highness of my tone. I'm reeling with anger, which is hard to set aside for confusion.

Furthermore, I usually supply my bank details for the hotels I work with.

They don't process my credit card since they pay me.

"Yes. Um." Papers ruffle before she continues. "I processed the hold for your reservation this evening, but the extras added to the booking last minute aren't going through. The florist said—"

"Florist?" I've not been handed a single flower since the day I wed. Roy said they were a waste of money and that he'd rather buy me a rose bush to plant so his gift could live on like our love.

What a crock of shit.

"Yes." She sounds even more nervous. "The petals on the bed are complimentary with the honeymoon suite, but if you want the arrangements you ordered from our florist, I will need to cite your card as I did during check-in."

Since I am silent, swimming in an abyss of fury, she assumes I am angry at her.

"I am sorry for the inconvenience, but the order was a little over a thousand dollars. I could have tried to push through the sale if it was under that. But—"

"It's okay," I assure her, my voice re-found and my wish for revenge surging. "You need to view my card in person, right?"

"Uh-huh." Now she's worried. "I could send someone to your room—"

"No!" I shout a little too loudly, startling Tempy. "My husband is showering, and I don't want you to..."

I've got nothing. Roy has the very definition of a dad bod, just minus the kids required for the title. My arms wobbled when I waved him goodbye this morning, but their flaps were barely noticeable when his turkey gobbler got stuck in a wind funnel.

Remembrance of the way he breezed out of our home this morning catapults my anger.

Did he know then that he was serving me divorce papers this evening?

When my head screams a resounding yes, I veer down the slippery slope of revenge instead of taking the high road.

"I'll be right down. Just give me a few minutes to get dressed. We barely made it into the suite before we started tearing our clothes off each other."

Her gag is audible. It is all the proof I need that she hasn't mixed up my husband's reservation with another man. "Wonderful. I'll see you soon."

I farewell her before opening my recently called list and copying and pasting her number into the Safari app. It shows the details of a hotel built in the last twelve months.

It is fancy but not as expensive as its counterparts since it is miles from the strip, which is odd since its advertisement continually states it is "discreet for *all* guests."

As my eyes bounce between the hotel's no-pet policy and Tempy, I try to think of a solution. Tempy loves our home as much as I do, but I don't trust Roy enough not to wonder if this is a ploy for him to dognap my beloved baby.

I'd hand over everything I own without a single gripe if he granted me full custody of Tempy.

Roy knows this, so I can't leave myself vulnerable to attack.

A smirk tilts my top lip when a brilliant idea smacks into me. "Do you want to go see Nanny?"

Mrs. Gessler loves Tempy. She spoils her rotten with homemade dog biscuits and often buys her bones bigger than her tiny frame. She's offered to babysit Tempy numerous times in the past six years, so I'm sure she'd love to babysit Tempy for an hour or two this evening.

When Tempy barks before spinning in a circle, I collect her leash from the coat rack, stuff my feet into the only heels in the coat room, and then race through the frosted glass door of my home like the bottom half of my outfit isn't impersonating dental floss.

2

MIRANDA

*T*empy is with Mrs. Gessler. Roy's outstanding bill was paid with the debit card he failed to tell me about when we merged assets, and I'm so burned up with adrenaline that no matter how large I make the gap in my coat, I feel seconds from death by dehydration.

It's winter! Did Vegas not get the memo?

When the elevator arrives on the floor of the honeymoon suite, I dip my chin in farewell to the man who entered with me in the lobby before I slowly exit.

Air whistles from his nose when he takes a final gawk of my six-inch-high stilettoes. The shoes I haven't worn since Valentine's Day three years ago have him convinced I am a paid escort.

No, I'm not hypothesizing.

He asked me my hourly rate before stumbling out that he'd double the fee the guest I was about to visit paid *and* purchase him a replacement escort so there'd be no hard feelings.

"Though I doubt I'll ever find him someone as tempting as you," he said while trying to woo me with both money and a confidence boost. "Perhaps I should send him a handful of the women who liaise with the guests here every evening?"

That's when it dawned on me why this hotel is so exclusive.

Not every room is booked out at a nightly rate.

Some are reserved per hour.

The swirls the knowledge hit my stomach with should have been my cue to leave. I wouldn't have hesitated if I hadn't recalled the prenuptial agreement Roy had me sign an hour before we exchanged vows. He is ten years my senior, so at the time, he was also more successful than me.

Our prenup is extremely in favor of him.

There's only one way I can tip the needle.

I need solid proof that he is having an affair. An infidelity clause was the only one I got approved.

Now I know why Roy fought so hard to have it expunged.

From the noises bellowing out of the honeymoon suite as I approach it, I'm mere seconds from securing enough proof to bury Roy and his unfair marriage contract.

With my body temp too high to function normally, I undo the final button of my trench coat and fan it open before I swipe the room keycard across the electronic lock.

It buzzes green for half a second before I push down on the latch.

I remain quiet, not wanting to startle Roy into an amicably neutral pose a divorce attorney could construe as friendly.

The honeymoon suite is massive. A living room with a grand

piano hogs most of the space, only slightly overshadowed by a mini kitchen squashed against one wall.

I understand its minuscule design. Who wants to cook when on their honeymoon? I certainly wasn't interested. Roy was just too cheap to mimic my logic.

The reminder of his stingy ways has me increasing the length of my strides. I dart through the living room, giving the opulence only a small snippet of attention before taking the spiral staircase that leads to the loft two stairs at a time.

The landing of the primary suite is gorgeous, with a working fireplace and Egyptian silks. I can't enjoy it, though, since the moans of a man in the midst of ecstasy are weakening its luxuriousness.

I also don't have a second to spare. Roy isn't known for his stamina.

With my iPhone held in front of me, recording every step I take, I burst into the main room of the primary suite and then jackknife my upper body toward a monstrous four-poster bed.

"You cheating piece of shit..."

My words trail off when I find a bed in pristine, untouched condition. The rose petals the check-in clerk mentioned earlier are scattered across the unrumpled bedding, and a bottle of champagne is cooling in a bucket of ice, but not a single person can be seen.

A god, though. There's one of them.

He isn't on the bed. He's sitting in a wingback chair on my left, snarling like I'm breaking into his apartment instead of the honeymoon suite my philandering husband booked for a weekend fuck-fest with his mistress.

The clerk tried to act nonchalantly while requesting ID to confirm that I was the Mrs. Martin she checked in a couple of hours ago.

The world's best actor would have had difficulty schooling her features while matching my license with the video footage of a barely legal blonde with legs that go for miles cozied up to Roy's side.

The clerk remade my card as requested before announcing she has security on standby if I require assistance, but the majority of the "busted on camera" stunt I hoped to pull off was left to me.

After numerous swallows, I ask, "Is this... I..."

I can't talk. I needed a bit of wetness to subdue the dryness the stranger's deliriously handsome face inspired, but spit is pooling in my mouth like an endless river.

My drooling can't be helped. The stranger is stunning in a way that demands a stupor state. His hair is dark, his eyes are light, and tattoos skate the thick lines of his arms and peek out the top of his rolled-up-at-the-sleeves dress shirt.

Since his eyes are scanning my body as adeptly as mine are drinking him in, I take my time assessing all his favorable points.

His rigid jawline is covered with wiry black scruff, his buttoned-up shirt is undone to just below a pendant on a thick chain, and over two dozen tattoos are on his left arm alone.

His attire is pricy and his shoes are designer, but his neck tattoos give him a risky edge a Vegas businessman would struggle to pull off. He screams dangerous. Murderer, even, but I can't stop staring.

I've never had the pleasure of standing across from such a

sexy, alluring man, and I don't want to give up a single second of ogling to consider an emotion as pitiful as fear.

This stranger deserves his own category of hot.

He is above and beyond the drool and flame emojis.

When the stranger coughs, forcing my eyes back to his panty-wetting face, I hook my thumb to the lower level of the suite. "Sorry. Ah." *Get with the program, Miranda.* "Is this the honeymoon suite?"

The door buzzed green before I entered.

I'm certain it did.

Unless it was unlocked, and I was burned up with too much anger to pay attention to the color of a flickering light.

I stop hyperfixating on how easy it is to get trampled when you're hell-bent on revenge when the stranger answers my question. "This *is* the honeymoon suite."

Even his voice is sexy. It is a mix of Russian and American, and it rolls over my skin like liquid ecstasy before minimizing my thigh gap. *Like it could get any smaller.*

"One of four on this floor alone."

My eyes pop as my throat works hard to swallow. "Oh. I'm so sorry. I have the wrong room."

I choke on my spit when the stranger replies in a way I never anticipated. "No, you don't."

He stands, doubling the output of my heart. He's tall, easily six foot four, and the span of his shoulders is even more imposing since they're no longer forced into the curved design of the overpriced armchair.

I watch in suspense as he moves closer. Each timed step doubles the output of my heart. I won't mention the surge of pulses to the lower half of my body, or you'll force me to sign Roy's divorce proposal without pause for thought.

I'm close to doing that without prompting. I'd give everything to pretend he didn't exist for an hour, to forget I ever agreed to marry him.

I would even be willing to make out I was the only one who broke the infidelity clause of our prenup.

That's how much this stranger's presence spikes my blood pressure and has me thinking recklessly.

I'm not the only one feeding off the tension. I suck in a desperate breath when the stranger's clipped demand breaks through the deep pounding of my pulse in my ears. "Knees. Now."

"Huh?"

I cough and splatter before scanning the plush carpet indented by the shoes I hid from Roy so he couldn't suggest I wear them again.

My blisters lasted longer than his combined efforts in the bedroom the entire time we've been together.

"Did you lose something?" I blubber when nervous, and it is showcased in the worst way. "I once lost a contact lens at a wedding ceremony. It was an intimate affair, but not even an hour of searching on my hands and knees could find it. I wouldn't have bothered if I didn't need it to drive home. I don't wear contacts because I want different-colored eyes like some peeps. I need them to see."

I take in the quickest breath. I'm not breathless because I speak in run-on sentences. It is from how close the stranger stands when he meets me at the entryway of the primary suite and how his eyes are even more fascinating up close. They're like a frozen pond in the Alps in the middle of winter. Fascinatingly unique.

When he smirks like he knows the reason for the heat in my cheeks, he says, "I didn't lose anything."

"You didn't?"

"Nope." The p in his reply pops and sends a rush of excitement to my core.

I wait and wait and wait for him to continue.

He does, but it isn't close to what I am anticipating.

"But you did."

Air hisses through his teeth as rapidly as mine when he flicks back half of my coat to expose the outfit I had hoped would milk my husband of one measly orgasm.

That's all I wanted—one climax with the hope it would help me survive another three hundred and sixty-five days of misery.

That's done with now.

Shitty moods, spiraling depressive episodes, and under-handed fatphobia comments I can handle. But booking a hotel and checking in with your mistress at the same time a competitor's firm serves your wife divorce papers is above my caliber of understanding.

It is our anniversary!

Who does that? Who cheats and serves papers on your wedding anniversary?

Don't take my anger the wrong way. The odds were stacked against us from the start. We weren't compatible.

Roy likes to go to bed early and wake up before the sparrows.

I like staying up late and sleeping in.

Roy prefers savory.

I'm obsessed with sweets.

Roy hates foreplay.

I'm beginning to forget what it means.

We're the opposite, and this time, opposites don't attract.

When the stranger's delicious scent flares my nostrils, I close my eyes and wish to become a fake-it-until-I-make-it girl.

Roy's lack of upper body strength means there's no possibility of pretending I'm with someone who won't grunt to his release in less than thirty seconds.

His stinky pits would give him away in an instant, not to mention how he only pumps three or four times before he stills.

This man would fuck for hours. I'm certain of it. Just the scent of his heated-up skin raises my blood pressure to a level it's never reached when bedded by Roy.

"Open your eyes," the stranger demands a short time later, his gruff tone sending a current down my spine.

When my eyes open and lock, I follow his murky eyes' lazy trek of my body. He starts at my chest before lowering them to my squidgy stomach.

Not once does disgust cross his face when he takes in how generously my curves fill the sexy mesh-and-rope design of my teddy. He drinks in my chunky thighs like he knows their sturdiness is an asset, not a downside, and the heat of his gaze makes me feel beautiful for the first time in a long time.

With my thoughts reckless, I try to find an out. "I should go."

"You should. But you won't." Lust hardens in his eyes as he repeats his earlier request. "Knees. Now."

When his hand gets lost in my mess of curls and he makes a fist, reality dawns.

He believes the same as my elevator co-rider.

He thinks I'm a paid escort.

"I'm not—"

He cuts me off by tugging on my locks firm enough to force me to my knees. "Don't speak."

His hold is aggressive, and it should sound sirens, but all it does is entice excitement. He likes what he sees, and it reminds me that, at one stage, I was seen as desirable.

Roy once said my sass was one of my most desired assets, so I use that against the stranger making me have wild, reckless thoughts. "I have pepper spray."

His smile is a mix of dangerous and sexy. "Where?"

As he wets his lips, he forces my knees apart with a gentle kick. His tap exposes the reason I picked this teddy. It is crotch-less, meaning it wouldn't have taken Roy longer to undress me than it would have for him to fuck me.

"I can't see a single weapon of destruction." Desire runs rampant through my veins, making it hard for me to breathe when he murmurs, "I see a fuck ton of them."

Again, his eyes trail down my breasts and across my flabby tummy before they land on the apex of my pussy. He smirks when he spots my wish to clamp my legs shut in the shake of my thighs. Then he doubles their fight.

"Did you wax today, or is it something you do on a regular basis?"

A reply leaves my mouth before I can stop it. "I used hair-removing cream."

"What was that?"

He heard me. The throbbing of the gigantic rock behind his zipper announces this, much less the relief blistering through his unique eyes. But for some reason, he wants me to repeat myself like whiny women with low self-esteem aren't his jam.

"I used hair-removing cream," I repeat more firmly. "*Because he would have used a recent waxing appointment as an excuse to turn me down.*"

I thought I said my last sentence in my head.

The stranger proves otherwise. "He?"

A snippet of doubt creeps under my skin.

Although I've yet to meet a man who isn't an adulterer, they seem to hate it when it is the woman being promiscuous.

After a quick exhale to free nerves from my voice, I raise my eyes to the stranger and then confess, "My husband."

"Your husband turns you down?"

He arches a brow when I nod but remains quiet. The silence should lessen the intensity of the tension brewing between us. It doesn't. It turns scalding, and within minutes, I am burning up everywhere.

My clit is thumping, and I'm wet enough for the scent of lust to overtake the anger leaking from my pores.

It's been years since I've felt this desired, but is that enough of an excuse to pardon the sanctity of my vows? My head screams no, but my body won't hear its claims.

My body wants to betray Roy as much as my heart does, and the stranger offers the perfect method of betrayal.

"Take my dick out."

I stammer, shocked. "Wh-what?"

He tightens his grip on my hair, exciting me further. "If you want to get back at the conniving two-faced dog you *once* called your husband, take my dick out."

My hands shoot for his belt before my brain can fire a single objection. Energy crackles in the air over my submissiveness. I don't know who is more turned on by it: the stranger or me.

My trek across Vegas was founded on revenge, so my readiness makes sense.

Hot breaths bound off the massive rod scarcely contained by the zipper of his pricy trousers, and they grow in intensity when I unbutton the top fastener and lower the zipper.

The more I fumble, the harder the stranger gets.

This is so left field for me that I feel like I'm drunk.

I honestly forgot how intoxicating lust can be.

The idea of sucking him off sends a tremor rolling down my spine, but still, nerves are present.

"I don't know what I'm doing."

"Yeah, you do," the stranger counters.

My heart catapults into my stomach when he uses his free hand to tug his pants and boxer shorts down his tattooed thighs, and his cock springs free. It is thick and veiny, leaking with pre-cum. It proves I'm not the only one turned on by my risqué tiptoe into enemy territory.

Wet heat floods my pussy when he fists the end of his shaft with his large hand. He's big and long, and even with my head shouting for me to tell him I'm not a prostitute, I wet my lips in preparation to be stretched.

His head tilts as a smile ghosts his mouth. As he stares straight at me, he slides his hand to the crown of his fat cock before he drags it back to the base. I shudder, on the verge of climax. I've never seen such a raw, primal act of masculinity in my life.

I draw in ragged breaths as I watch the stranger pump his cock for several long strokes.

Watching isn't cheating. Roy has claimed that several times over the past fourteen years.

Even if it were, the visual is too enticing not to gawk at.

My theory that I'm not cheating goes out the window when the stranger rolls his thumb over the slit at the tip of his cock so he can transfer a droplet of pre-cum to my lips.

When his thumb breaches between my lips, my insides squeeze. He tastes delicious, and it sets a fire ablaze in my core—a fire I can't control.

Shit, I'm going to come if I don't calm the wildfire spreading across my midsection.

The effort to hold back the sensation I've not experienced in an extremely long time doubles when the stranger mutters, "Not yet. You're not allowed to come yet." Disappointment stops blistering my skin when he adds, "You're not allowed to come until you're riding my face or strangling my cock. So what is it going to be, *printsessa*? Do you want to take me for a ride, or are you reserving the pleasure for me?"

I look at him, lost.

Why is it my choice? My wants didn't factor in with Roy. We did missionary once a month until eighteen months ago. Foreplay was rarely an option. When it was, it was never about me.

"Christ," grunts out the stranger. "The innocence in your eyes doesn't match the sexiness of your body. I've never been more desperate."

Sexy? Does he think I'm sexy?

My imaginary Victoria's Secret angel feathers fan out to their full wingspan when he says, "So make your choice, *printsessa*, because I sure as fuck ain't coming until you've screamed my name at least twice."

"I'd have to know your name to scream it."

Shock barely registers from the bluntness of my reply. How could it when nothing but sheer awe flares through his eyes from my sassiness?

"Nero, baby. My name is Nero." He slides his hand up and down his densely veined shaft a handful of times before he murmurs, "But you can call me whatever the fuck you want while riding my face. Daddy. God. A seat with no arms. The choice is yours." His groan when his eyes lower to the crotchless region of my teddy is my undoing. I want him now more than my lungs crave air. "So how about you get your fine ass on the bed and spread your legs for me. Let me see exactly what I'm about to feast on."

"I—"

"I ain't asking, *printsessa*." His tone is threatening but also not. It is as if he is used to getting his way, but he enjoys being challenged. "My hard-earned money paid for this room, so I want the full shebang of my spend."

Since my last snippet of sass was well-received, I give it another try. "Isn't it the pro's job to make sure her john is taken care of?" He smirks again and then nods. "Then how about you shut up and let me work my magic?"

3

MIRANDA

"Fuck. Me." Pre-cum leaks from Nero's cock as he walks backward, his eyes never leaving mine. "Knew it wouldn't take long to find what you lost. Never expected it to be this fast, though."

When there is a safe distance between us, I should hightail it for the exit and write off our exchange as a near miss. But since I'm feeling things I haven't felt in a long time, and I'm just as confident they'll be lost again within minutes of me leaving, I slowly cross the room.

My thighs rub during my last two strides, but there's no friction. I'm too soaked from how thick Nero's cock becomes the longer he watches me under hooded lids. He's as hard as an iron rod, and his body's response to my prance surges more than my libido.

My confidence is just as high.

I'm almost at the bed when Nero says, "Lose the coat."

I hesitate. Confidence is an entirely different matter when you have coverage.

Without it, I will wither like a picked flower.

"Y-you first," I demand, breathing heavily.

Slickness extends beyond the barrier of my crotchless teddy when his hands move to the done-up buttons on his dress shirt without hesitation.

This is when I notice the tattoos on his hands extend to his fingers. They're a combination of symbols, letters, and numbers, and they send my head into a tailspin.

I've always thought tattoos were sexy. Roy said they were only for gangbangers. I still haven't told him about the butterfly on my inner thigh. I got it in rebellion, and although I've been barely seen out of sweats ever since, that isn't the sole cause of his unawareness.

He'd have to grant me more than five seconds of attention to notice anything, much less an object I'm purposely hiding from him.

I blink up at Nero when the last button is undone. He takes his time removing his shirt from his bulky shoulders like he too believes undressing is the longest part of any sexual encounter.

I'd be worried if he didn't seem the type with a heap of stamina.

With his pants already huddled around his tattooed thighs, it doesn't take longer than ten seconds for him to remove them. It would have been instantaneous with his shirt if he didn't need to toe off his shoes.

As I drink in endless lines of ink and muscles, he tosses his shirt and pants onto the armchair he was seated on when I burst into his life.

Muscles I didn't know existed pop when he steps closer. "Your turn."

Not waiting for me to fathom a reply, much less answer him, he tugs on the lapels of my trench coat and guides it off my shoulders. Its whoosh when it floats to the floor matches the hiss that leaves his mouth when my breasts are fully exposed.

I'm one of those full-breasted girls.

I didn't get just cleavage and a bit of side boob.

I got the works.

Nero likes what he sees and has no qualms about sharing his thoughts. "I knew your tits would be fantastic. I can't wait to taste them."

I thrust out my chest as if to say, *Then what are you waiting for?*

Nero's husky laugh does wild things to my insides. "If I taste them, I'll want to taste your pussy immediately after."

"And that's a problem because?"

My thighs clench when he mutters, "Because I need to start here first." He drags his thumb over my bone-dry lips. "Before I move to here." My nipples are awarded his attention next. "Then I'll finish here." I pant when his finger slips between the folds of my pussy. I'm wet, so he doesn't face an ounce of resistance. "Fuck." His one word is rough and unhinged, the very essence of a man on the brink of release. "You're already drenched for me."

When he peers down at me, lust snatches the last of my apprehension. I launch at him, propelling myself onto my tippy-toes. Our lips brush, and a moan vibrates through my chest. I don't know if it came from Nero or me, but it sets off a frenzy of grunts, moans, and teasing licks.

There's nothing sweet about our kiss. Nothing childish. It is the embrace of lust, and it makes me the wettest I've ever been.

As Nero's fingers again get lost in my hair, I scrape the back of his head with my nails and draw him closer. It is a rough kiss, full of passion and driven by need.

In seconds, we're on the mattress, tangled in a mess of legs and arms. Nero grinds against an area damp enough to need a Slippery When Wet sign displayed while I bury my face into his neck.

It's hard to remain hidden when his lips lower to my breast. There's no coverage, and I can't help but stare.

He sucks my nipple into his mouth, arching my back before he swirls his tongue around the puckered nub.

"Fucking divine." He adds a scrape of his teeth this time before he shifts his focus to my left breast. "Your tits are perfect."

After enough attention to have me dripping, his mouth lowers several inches. I try to encourage him straight to my pussy, hopeful a hurried shove will have him missing the rolls my stomach isn't without even when I lay as straight as an ironing board.

He won't allow it.

As he pinches my nipple, sending a yelp bouncing around the room, his tongue traces the lines the teddy marked my skin with before he spears it inside my belly button.

That has me moaning.

I had no clue my belly button was an erogenous zone.

I breathe heavily when Nero's tongue finds the edge of my crotchless teddy. His fingers look prepared to travel the same route as his tongue, but something deviates their attention.

"This is sexy." He runs a calloused fingertip over the butterfly tattoo on my inner thigh before playfully grazing it with his teeth. My readiness smears his cheek. That's how hidden my tattoo is. You have to splay my thighs wide open to see it. No man has ever bothered to get that close and personal with me. "I think you need one here as well."

He bites at the delicate skin on my opposite thigh, sending another yelp bouncing around the room before he looks up at me.

He stares while pushing a finger inside me to the first knuckle, gauging my response.

I whimper.

It isn't in fear.

It is in desperation.

We suck in a combined breath when he slides his finger out before he increases its burn by giving the solo traveler a girthy counterpart.

He pushes two fingers in deep, loving the desperate search of my hands to claw something. They scratch the bedding before bunching it into firm balls. My moans are nowhere near as controllable. They barrel out of me like waves crashing to shore.

I moan, cuss, and grunt as Nero continues to unravel me with his fingers. He pumps them in and out of me for several long minutes before he rolls his thumb over my clit.

That's my undoing.

I come with a hoarse cry, shuddering and shaking through my first climax in over three years.

And then his mouth is on me.

"No," is the first thought to leave my head, and then, "More. Please. Oh god."

My hand flies up to clamp my mouth when Nero eats me with an expertise I've never experienced. He curls his tongue around my clit and grazes it with his teeth while finger fucking me at a leisured yet mind-spiraling pace.

I groan and rock my hips upward, mashing my pussy with his mouth. All quests for revenge are lost, my focus now solely on the present. I'm not Miranda, a soon-to-be divorcee. I am sexy and wanted and being eaten by the most handsome man I've ever laid eyes on.

Every muscle clenches as I come again.

I bite on the palm of my hand, silencing the franticness of my screams when Nero doesn't stop.

His tongue doesn't stop slithering.

His fingers don't still.

He continues fucking me with his mouth and hand until not even the most painful bite will stop my moans from bellowing down the hotel's hallway.

Nero's tongue finally leaves my clit half a second before he looms above me. I feel the pulse of his cock when he braces it at the opening of my pussy. His groan when he feels the results of my multiple climaxes tightens my core.

I'm drenched front to back and barely coherent, but not even a near-comatose state would have me missing how far his cock stretches.

It braces against my pussy and halfway up my stomach.

I veer my eyes from his impressive cock when he says, "Can you bury the urge to hide from me if I take you like this, or do I need to change positions?"

Embarrassment that he knows my neurosis barely graces my cheeks; however, Nero acts as if they are on fire.

Without a single struggle, he switches our position until I'm hovering above him and he's sprawled beneath me. He licks his lips as his eyes travel down my body. When he tastes me on his mouth, it reminds him of his early offer for me to ride his face.

He shimmies down like it isn't a tight squeeze for a man of his size to fit between my thighs before he bands his arms around my legs and arrows his head toward my drenched slit.

"It's okay. I don't need—"

Holy mother of god.

One flick of my clit with his nose and I come.

I don't make a sound. It is silent but strong enough to almost pull my knees out from beneath me.

I hold back, not wanting to suffocate Nero.

Once the tingles racing through my veins dissipate, I try to dismount.

Nero holds on strong.

"Not yet." His heated breaths batter my overstimulated clit. "You haven't even taken your seat yet, so the show isn't close to starting, much less finishing." He tugs me down, growling when my thighs hug his ears and cheeks. "Fuck yes, *printsessa*. Ride my face."

My body is shaking so much it is hard to move, but Nero guides me. With his tattooed fingers digging into my thick thighs, he guides me back and forth and back and forth until stars commence blistering for the umpteenth time.

"That's it. Just like that. Come over my mouth."

As his breathy words batter my clit, I climax again.

My body shakes and quivers, and I lose control of my legs.

Nero doesn't seem to mind. His grip is almost bruising as he forces me entirely onto his mouth. He awards me with a heap of praise that prolongs the length of my orgasm before he rubs his cheek over the cleft of my pussy, absorbing my scent.

I'm so strung out on lust that I barely register him moving me until his hot steel rod rubs at the opening of my pussy, coating itself in my arousal. I'm on top, so I should have all the control, but I don't need to do a thing.

Nero lines up before he drives home, impaling me with one ardent thrust.

"Fuck."

I can't express words. I can barely breathe. The stretch is painful, and the burn of taking someone with a heap of girth is a first.

"Not yet," he snaps out again when I attempt to move. "Need you to acclimate first."

"I'm fine. I am drenched. You can move."

I'm full.

So fucking full.

But it feels too good to worry about a slight snippet of pain.

"Please move."

My plea comes out desperate, and Nero immediately answers it. He slides his cock almost all the way out by hoisting me up as if I don't weigh a thing before he yanks me back down.

I moan, a better response above me.

"That's it," Nero murmurs when my mewl reaches his ears. "Take my cock like a good little wifey."

I stab my nails into his tattooed chest before encouraging an increase in speed. I slam down as his hips jerk upward, our bodies slapping from their brutal collision.

"Again." His fingers flex on my hips as his cock throbs. "Ride my cock like you did my face. Take me to the very base. Swallow every inch of the monster dick your sexy-ass curves caused."

His movements get more precise, and his thrusts become more urgent.

He fucks me as much as I fuck him, and it lasts forever.

"It's good. So, so good."

My thighs cuddle his as I rock my hips forward with every pump. I grind against him, dampening more with every rub of my clit against his V muscle.

We rock in sync for several long minutes, tiring both my body and my mental capacity.

"I need you to come again, *printsessa*. I need you to come now because you feel so good wrapped around my cock. I'm not sure how much longer I can hold back."

Knowing he's close to the brink spreads a smile across my face.

He hasn't taken his eyes off me for a single second—not once.

The knowledge that he likes what he sees is thrilling, and I feed off the confidence it awards me.

When Nero drinks in my smile, his expression turns serious.

"Even more so now." As his grip on my waist tightens, he says,

"We need to change positions. It's time for me to fuck you how you deserve to be fucked."

I squeal when he maneuvers me as if I am as light as a feather. Then I scream when he enters me from behind.

I have no clue how we didn't get twisted up in a sticky, sexy mess. I went from riding his cock from above to being on my hands and knees, taking him from behind.

"Deep. You're so deep," I murmur when he takes me deep enough for his balls to slap my clit.

Nero spanks my right butt cheek, sending heated tingles across the surface of my skin. "Your ass..." A groan ends his sentence before he spanks me again, harder this time. It's firm enough to leave a mark, but ludicrously, I'm not worried.

Roy filed for divorce, so technically, this isn't cheating.

Even if it is, it is too late now.

Nero has had his tongue, fingers, and cock inside me, and if I have it my way, his sperm is next.

I squeeze around Nero's fat cock when he bands his arm around my body to toy with my clit. He multitasks like a pro. He drives into me on repeat while rubbing and caressing my swollen clit.

He also bombards me with a heap of praise.

He tells me my body is a temple and that it deserves to be worshipped. That a woman as sexy and beautiful as me should never cover up with dowdy clothes and oversized sweats. He adores my curves and encourages what he assures me are sexy moves by making them dance in sync with the fluent flexes of the muscles covering every inch of his delectable body.

"Come for me again, *printsessa*," he demands while cramming his cock inside me.

His cock flexes when it bottoms out at my uterus, and then he relishes the tight squeezes of my vaginal walls when I give in to the sensation turning me into a blubbering, shuddering mess.

I come with a loud cry, Nero's name ripping from my lips.

Again, Nero doesn't stop, slow, or come.

He lets me enjoy the moment of being first for a change before he finally loosens the restraints he's barely controlling.

He thrusts in deep and then stills so my pussy can milk his cock one last time.

"Christ," he grunts through clenched teeth as cum spurts from his cock.

I smirk at the exhaustion in his tone before slowly sinking into the mattress. I'm zonked, yet exhaustion isn't weighing down my eyelids. I feel the most alive I've ever felt.

When rustling sounds from behind, I crank my neck back. Nero is edging off the bed. His cock is glistening with our combined arousal.

That's when it dawns on me that we forgot to use protection.

"I'm on the pill," I blurt out like it is an automatic shield for STIs. "I take it religiously." I lift my eyes from a cock still larger than any I've seen, even with it in the process of deflating, and lock them with a lust-filled pair. "But I can take Plan B if it will ease your conscience."

Nero's smile has me on the cusp of ecstasy again. "It's fine. I trust you."

That's ballsy for him to say considering I confessed at the start of our exchange that I'm married.

Nero drinks in my shock for half a second before he lowers his eyes to the nonexistent crotch of the teddy. "Let me get something to clean you up."

There's no shame to his words, no color of embarrassment heating his cheeks, but it is still a fight not to scamper for some coverage when he heads to the bathroom.

He's all muscles and ink, and I'm soft and flabby.

We are *not* the same.

As Nero enters the bathroom, I sling my eyes to a mirror in the corner of the room. The angle is off. I can't check if I have raccoon eyes and bird's nest hair, so I scoot off the mattress and tiptoe across the plush carpet.

Three seconds later, I glance into the mirror, taking in my flushed cheeks, dilated eyes, and messy mop of curls.

Instead of grimacing, I feel heat slick my skin.

My choice of lingerie is even more risqué now since it is caressing impassioned, lust-spurred skin. I feel beautiful and uplifted—two things I hadn't considered experiencing today.

A faucet shutting off shifts my focus. I head back for the bed, not wanting to look like an unconfident fool—or worse, a cocky airhead.

I make it halfway back before a groan stops me in my tracks.

I recognize that moan.

It's beaten me to the finish line dozens of times over the past fourteen years but never lingered long enough for me to mimic it.

"Roy?" I murmur while moving closer to the closet at the far side of the room.

This hotel is new, but it has louver doors that were the rage from the '50s until the '80s. The slats on this one are mostly open, and the shadow my horniness hid earlier is human-sized.

With my heart in my throat, I lock eyes with the glossy pair peering at me through a louver before carefully prying open the door.

When I find Roy in the closet, my hand shoots up to muffle my squeal. He's bound to a chair, and his almost naked frame is covered with a range of bruises and cuts. His eyes are wet and wide, and the red lettering scoured across his forehead wasn't there when he left home this morning.

Cheater.

I'm not given the chance to fret. The photographs scattered beneath his shoeless feet warrant nothing less than pure rage. They show Roy in a range of positions. All of them are sexual, and I don't feature in a single one of them.

My eyes dart up from an image of Roy tied to a bed that looks oddly similar to our marital bed when he grunts and groans as if possessed.

My body registers the cause of his alarm in his bloodshot eyes half a second before the voice of a man who brought me to climax more times in the past hour than I've achieved myself over the past three years confirms it.

"I planned to kill him."

When I twist to face Nero, he dumps a damp washcloth and props his shoulder on the bathroom doorjamb before folding his thick arms in front of his chest. His stance displays the aggression in his tone has nothing to do with me, and everything to do with my husband.

"I was in the process of doing precisely that when you interrupted us. Then I figured *this* would hurt him more." He thrusts his hand between us during the *this* part of his reply.

As I struggle to work out what he means, he pushes off the doorjamb to fetch his pants from the foot of the bed. I watch him with eagle eyes as he gets dressed. He moves with such fluency that it is as if I am attending a Broadway show. I can't take my eyes off him.

Once his cock is concealed and he's absently placed on his shirt, Nero lifts his eyes from the surveillance images scattered around Roy's feet to my face. He features in as many of the surveillance images as I do—not at all—but the ticking of his jaw makes it obvious the tall, slender blonde draped across Roy in multiple pictures is known to him.

"I don't know what pissed me off the most. My soon-to-be ex-wife thinking she could take me to the cleaners by sucking her divorce attorney's cock, or her assumption I wouldn't find out she secured the best divorce attorney in Vegas *before* I filed." He rakes my body with a hooded gaze, almost making it seem as if we're lucky our spouses chose to cheat with each other. "Neither point mattered once you arrived. One glance and I realized I hadn't lost anything." He snarls at Roy as he crosses the room. "He won't be so lucky."

Roy is gagged with his own stinky sock, so his mumbles make no sense, but two words make it through the chaos. "Run, Miranda!"

I glare at him like he's insane before shaking my head. I can't get my legs to move. They're not frozen in fear. They're exhausted from endless orgasms and growing more wary the longer Nero stares. His eyes are pumping out a range of emotions. I pay attention to the sheer ownership in them the most.

Before I can overthink how quick I am to trust a stranger, Nero's fingers knot into my curls, and he tugs my head back. A sliver of silver catches my attention. It is obvious the switchblade Nero is clutching is the cause of Roy's fret. His pupils are massive, and I can smell his stinky armpits from here.

He thinks Nero is going to hurt me.

I don't feel the same way.

I'm the prey and Nero is the hunter, but this game was over the instant he stuffed me to the brim with his big, fat cock.

"Ah," Nero murmurs when he notices my lack of fear. "I got your title mixed up." He inches closer, fanning my lips with his heated breaths. "You're not a princess." Heat burns through me when he says, "You're a queen."

My heart stops beating when his lips arrow toward mine. Our noses brush before his tongue slides across my kiss-swollen mouth.

When my lips part at the request of his lashing tongue, he slides his tongue into my mouth and does a long, leisured lick.

My insides clench and my knees buckle when he kisses me like we don't have an audience, like my husband isn't bound, gagged, and injured mere feet from us.

His kiss matches his body.

It is godlike.

Only once I am again pliable from his touch does he pull back. Lust fires in the air when he inches back far enough to align our eyes and expose the winner's smirk tilting his plump lips at one side.

The victory flaring through his hooded gaze should hackle my last nerve, but somehow, it doesn't. He's right. I'm not a princess. I am the ruler of my realm, and it is time for me to take back my crown.

"It was a pleasure to meet you, Miranda."

He presses his lips to my temple and draws in a long breath before he places something cool and smooth into my palm.

I stare down at a switchblade.

"He will never get over watching his wife fuck like a thoroughbred." The cockiness fluffing out his peacock feathers dulls a smidge before he says, "But if you don't believe that punishment will make up for him sleeping with my wife, you're free to issue whatever sentence you deem fit."

He squeezes my hand holding the switchblade before moving to collect the jacket I didn't notice hanging in the closet Roy is hogging until now. He yanks out his designer jacket, grinning when the coat hanger snaps from his rueful tug. Its sharp edge adds another nick to Roy's bloody face.

"A cleanup crew will arrive in an hour. No matter what route you take, you have my word that they'll make it seem like you were never here."

Nero takes in Roy's shirtless torso and battered arms while he puts on his jacket. I should use the time to consider my options, but all I do is gawk.

"Cut him free or cut off his cock." His eyes are on me again, hot and narrowed. The latter point is for Roy. The former is for me. "I'm satisfied with the outcome I achieved today. Now the ball is in your court."

His eyes lower, and he groans when he notices the steady rise and fall of my chest.

After imprinting his lower lip with his teeth, he awards me with a frisky wink and then heads for the exit.

I wait for the bang of the honeymoon suite's door closing to boom up the stairwell before I shift on my feet to face Roy. He's hurting. There's no doubt about that. I don't believe all his pain centers on the cuts, the bruises, and the freshly inked tattoo scoured across his forehead, though.

What Nero said is true. He'll never get over seeing me with another man.

For once, my actions obliterated his ego, and I'm glad.

My confidence feeds off the wetness in his eyes when I walk toward him with a strut in my step. He's only witnessed it once since he cut it to pieces with a ton of cruel words.

The last time I wore lingerie, he told me I should dress appropriately for my body type, and someone "with too much fat on their bones" should steer clear of the lingerie section of the department store.

Another man's cum is dribbling down my thigh, but Roy doesn't pay it an ounce of attention. He's too focused on the trek of the switchblade I flicked open during my strut, sweating when I glide it up his thigh. He's never seen my eyes hold this much confidence. Unlike with Nero, the awakening of my self-assurance has him petrified.

"Mir..." he murmurs, his use of a nickname purposeful and with hope. He thinks he can play me for a fool again. I have news for him. "I made a mistake."

"A mistake? Ha!"

I stuff his sock in more profoundly, stealing his chance to issue more lies before positioning the switchblade between his splayed thighs. The rope circling his ankles isn't forcing a thigh gap. His legs are so skinny, even flattened on the chair, that not an ounce of fat spills over.

His middle leg is just as scrawny as its counterparts.

"Mir..." His mumble is fraught, full of distress. "Pleas—"

I silence him by yanking the switchblade upward, tethering far more than the sanctity of our vows with one swift slice.

He keeps his cock—just. But I'm hopeful the footage from the blinking red contraption propped at his right will help me strip anything of real value from his life.

4

NERO

*A*nger boils my blood when the annoying snivel of a woman with no class rustles through my ears. Tasha, my soon-to-be ex-wife, could be crying because she watched the commencement of the beatdown I gave the pathetic fuck who thought he could touch my property without permission and get away with it, but the weakness of her sobs and the lack of fire in her eyes announce a different scenario.

She isn't a woman in fear for her life.

She's jealous of the pure contentment on my face.

Serves her fucking right.

I'll never be classified as a gentleman—I've done too much time, too much blow, and too many women to stretch for unattainable goals—but from the moment we woke up in a penthouse apartment of one of the many Popov Vegas hotels with a platinum band wrapped around my finger and a freshly inked marriage certificate dumped on the pool table, I've kept my dick in my pants.

It was a fucking hard feat, but my ma raised me right.

She'd have my head just on the thought that I believed I could stray after marriage.

My father has many children to many women, so his third wife, who thought she was his first and *only* wife, did everything in her power to stop their only son from following in his footsteps.

Did her plan work? Hardly. But what Ma doesn't know won't hurt her.

Breathing is enticing. I'm fond of it, though I am confident weasels like Roy Martin aren't.

How could they be?

You don't tiptoe into hell and expect to leave without ash covering your feet.

As I slip into the front passenger seat of a sleek white sports car, the engine kicks over. Eight, the man steering both my vehicle of choice and my quest for revenge when he brought me the evidence I've been seeking for the past three weeks, seems eager to leave.

I'm not as raring. Revenge is still heating my veins, making them black, but only a clown would assist a butterfly with emerging from her cocoon and not stay to watch the expansion of her wings.

"Wait," I demand, my eyes unmoving from the hotel I just exited.

I entered to kill the man who thought he could play me for a fool.

One glance changed everything—both today and back then.

Even with half her body covered with a trench coat, I liked what I saw.

Very much so.

My cock hardens again as I recall how Miranda's ample curves were accentuated by the overtop lighting of the penthouse suite and how her beauty was undeniable in the tiny teddy incapable of concealing an inch of her cock-thickening curves.

As my eyes raked her body, my once seemingly unquenchable thirst for revenge switched to need. Roy had the epitome of perfection willing to accept his last name, yet he threw it away for the crumbs in the bottom of a cereal box no one wants to sog their milk.

Tasha is precisely what you'd expect to wake up next to after an all-night bender in a Vegas casino. Her features are sharp, her façade exudes bitchiness even while smiling, and she is so malnourished I doubt she's ever eaten a calorie-laden meal in her adult years.

She thinks attractiveness is rated on who has the lowest digits on both the scales and the tags of the designer dresses she racked up on my credit card within hours of us tying the knot.

For me, Tasha's size-zero logic spreads goose eggs across the board.

Zero personality.

Zero empathy.

And zero smarts when it comes to not biting the hand feeding her.

I didn't come close to sensing any of those things when I spotted Miranda. For the first time in a long time, a sense of calm washed over me as I stood across from a woman with more grace in her pinkie than Tasha has in her entire body.

The betrayal, the hurt, the utmost desire for revenge was all gone, stolen by the prospect that a woman as refined as Miranda didn't deserve to face the brunt of *their* betrayal alone.

You could see her confidence was beaten to hell. Her shoulders hung as obviously low as the defeated gleam clouding her pretty eyes.

Although I told myself time and time again that her anguish was not mine to mollify, I couldn't walk away. She was a beacon drawing me in and making me forget, and I went from aiming my gun at her head to stuffing it so deep into the armchair that I'll have to pay Roy a second visit once Miranda has left.

She doesn't have it in her to kill him. Yet.

I make no promises when the confidence I saw deep inside her months ago fully flourishes.

Not even I may survive that metamorphosis.

5

MIRANDA

*T*he cable I severed to save me from needing to crawl between Roy's legs to unplug the ancient camcorder sits between his shaky thighs more prominently than his shriveled dick.

He knows what this footage means.

It is my ticket to freedom.

As Roy's whines ramp up, his mumbles more sobs than pleas for forgiveness, I stuff my arms into the openings of my trench coat. The evidence of a marriage incapable of reconciliation is scattered around me, as undeniable as the droplets of cum dripping down my thighs.

Once I've tightened my coat around the teddy making me feel invincible, I search for my purse and phone. I swore I'd left them near the entry of the primary suite, but they are nowhere to be found.

A gun, though. There's one of them.

Panic hits me, and for a moment, a sense of disappointment.

Having Roy taken care of would be easier than playing him at a game he's perfected over the past twenty-plus years, but I don't think I'll ever see murder as the solution to any predicament.

With that in mind, I dump the gun onto the side table concealing my purse and phone before I grab my things and head for the door. My steps are firm and resolute.

The hallway is eerily quiet, the click of my heels against the polished floor the only sound.

I don't look back when I spy the man I rode the elevator with earlier a couple of doors down. I can't. He'll see my flushed face and think I duped my pimp out of a hefty payday.

The elevator ride to the lobby feels like an eternity, but I keep my head high, refusing to let the heaviness of my somewhat betrayal weigh heavily on my chest.

Roy cheated first, and can you really call it cheating when the mashup occurred *after* being served divorce papers?

As I step into the lobby, a cool blast of air from an overhead air-conditioning unit hits my face, giving welcomed relief to my blemished cheeks.

I walk through the foyer, acting oblivious as to the cause of the hotel receptionist's sympathetic smile.

I felt pathetic two hours ago, but those thoughts have now vanished, along with years of sexual frustration.

Outside, the city is alive and bustling, a similar resemblance to the feelings settling over me. I pause for a moment, taking it all in. This is the fresh start I've been seeking for the past fourteen years, and it is all thanks to him, Nero, the man across the street who's eyeballing me like my hair isn't a mess and my mascara isn't giving me raccoon eyes.

Like earlier, something in his gaze sets my skin on fire. It is a mix of admiration and disappointment, like he'd rather I be carrying Roy's testicles than the camcorder that will set me free, but that he also believes the injustice is only temporary.

The reminder of how greatly he built my courage with one exchange fuels my willpower. I lift my chin, determined to face whatever comes next with dignity and respect.

This is my life, and I'm taking it back.

My determination wilts like a picked flower on a windowsill only days later. I seize the damn bolts on the bed, but no amount of muscle will budge them.

This is the bed featured numerous times in the surveillance images circling Roy's bloodied feet, the one sullied by Roy and his mistress. I couldn't sleep on it even if I wanted to, but with the bolts refusing to budge, I may not have a choice.

The only other room in my home seconds as Roy's home office, and the sofa, although sexy, with big shiny buttons and leather trim, is horribly uncomfortable.

My back has been screaming all weekend.

When a third attempt on the bolt holding together the bulky wooden frame of the bed we purchased within days of returning from our honeymoon is fruitless, I blow a wayward hair out of my eye and slump onto the floor.

The wooden floorboards are as cold as the ice cream I am

denying myself of since I've forgotten Roy no longer has a say on what I do and do not eat.

I've had to hide anything above a zero-calorie rating for years, so it will take more than a couple of days to remember I no longer need to justify my food intake to a man who was meant to love me, warts and all.

"You're such an idiot," I chastise myself after recalling how perfectly slim Roy's surveillance camera partner was.

Her bones didn't hold an ounce of fat, and she was at least a decade younger than me.

I'd have to diet on lettuce only for a year to get close to her standard of the perfect figure.

I would have started days ago if my body weren't still humming in the aftermath of multiple orgasms. I didn't feel gross while standing across from Nero with my trench coat one dangerous flap from a nipple slip.

He made me feel my weight in gold, and I've yet to come down from the orgasmic high.

The reminder of my past few days of flightiness sees me dumping my pink wrench into the tool kit I purchased when the furnace needed servicing and clambering to the kitchen.

I rarely bake when I'm home. Roy's unapproving glares always overcooked the goodies he was adamant I should never consume.

But with the locks changed an hour after I returned from the hotel, and Tempy old enough to face the injustice of an oven cranking out heat for hours while living in the middle of a desert, I pull condiments out of my pantry and refrigerator before dragging over my KitchenAid freestanding mixer.

The past few days have been eye-opening, and not necessarily in a bad way. I've taken some time to reflect, collect evidence of Roy's philandering and seemingly allergic reaction to paying his share of our bills, and seek the assistance of a divorce attorney.

It's been good. I'm finding my feet relatively fast and am hopeful the stability I've discovered with single life continues on a relatively smooth track.

In a matter of hours, my kitchen switches from spotlessly clean to overrun with baked goods.

Baking is as natural as breathing for me. It was my first love. I wanted to open a bakery, but Roy steered me toward event catering instead. He said events such as weddings and bar mitzvahs attract a surcharge bakers would cream their pants to earn in a week, and that I'd be less tempted to sample the merchandise when surrounded by brides vying to fit into their size-zero dresses and mothers wanting to top the MILF rankings for their neighborhood.

I huff before loading ingredients from memory into the stainless-steel mixing bowl attached to the KitchenAid for the umpteenth time this afternoon.

I'm so used to catering for an audience that I triple the quantities without thinking. My small oven isn't handling the excess. It's been chugging along all afternoon, but it feels good to cook for happiness again instead of it seeming like a chore.

I splash a little Japanese whisky and yuzu into my current mix before taking a swig out of the almost empty bottle. It's sour enough to add a husky giggle to my words when I answer Tempy's silent reprimand with words. "It could be worse. I could have paired it with tequila."

When she remains staring with her adorable head slanted, I chug down another mouthful of yuzu before adding an extra dollop to the batter whirling around the bowl.

I'm on the cusp of tipsy with barely two sips, so you can imagine how bad my dizziness becomes when my doorbell rings.

Tempy is up on her feet in an instant, barking excitedly and racing for the door.

Panic swirls inside me for half a second before I straighten the rod in my spine by rolling back my shoulders.

Roy's betrayal didn't break me.

It made me stronger.

Furthermore, Tempy can't stand Roy. She growled when he forgot his keys and needed to knock. However, she's so excited right now she looks on the verge of making a mess on my recently mopped floor.

My strength has grown so stupendously over the past three days that I almost pull the door from the hinges when I yank it open.

"If you've *finally* come for your things, you're too late. I already donated them. A charity worker is collecting them first thing tomorrow morning." My sentence ends with a hiccup, my body as equally nervous as it is excited when I realize the person standing on the other side of the door isn't my cheating, low-life, soon-to-be ex. It is the man I am confident can make me forget him with nothing but a smirk. "Nero... Um. Hello."

While opening the door, wordlessly welcoming him into my home, I give my head a stern talking to. I'm not a blubbering underage idiot with no life experience. I am an independent woman... who could come just by looking at this man's deliriously handsome face.

Jesus, Mir. Get a grip!

After swishing my tongue around to encourage some wetness for the fire in my throat, I say, "Come in. Please."

I bite back a moan when he accepts my offer. He smells delicious, his scent a mixture of danger and tranquility. It is stronger than the goodies I've been baking over the past several hours and has me suddenly starving.

"That's Tempy," I introduce when she pops up on her hind legs to welcome Nero with half a dozen spins and paw waves. "She's a little starved of attention."

A deliciously immoral shiver rolls down my spine when Nero laughs while dragging his hand over Tempy's head. He tickles under her chin with his chunky tattooed fingers, making my skin slick with envy.

I squeeze my thighs together while recalling how wonderous his fingers are, now too feeling starved of attention I had no clue I craved so desperately until now.

6

NERO

The reason for my visit slips my mind when Miranda guides us toward her kitchen. She's dressed casually in leggings that show off every inch of her curves and an oversized shirt that does a shit job of covering up said curves since it is knotted in the middle of her stomach.

She's shoeless and sockless, and even if I hadn't heard her declaration while she ripped her door from its hinges, I'd still be aware she has no intention of taking back her cheating spouse.

Anything non-girlie and bulky has been packed and stored next to the entryway table. If the singe marks on the lawn, and the spitfire stubbornness in her eyes, are anything to go by, anything small and perishable is now soot.

My butterfly is still soaring high.

"Can I get you something to drink? Coffee? Water?" Miranda spins to face me, wafting a scent that is uniquely her. "Japanese whisky?"

When I shake my head, she shrugs before she downs a healthy mouthful from a bottle that retails in the high three hundreds.

With the twitching of her nose announcing the tingles racing across her plump lips, she checks the denseness of a yellow batter in a mixing bowl before switching off the mixer and transferring the ingredients into a circular pre-prepared cake tin.

"I bake when..." Lines sprout across her nose when her expression tightens into an adorable scowl. "I *used* to bake when depressed. It doesn't feel right saying that now."

When she gestures for me to sit across from her, I slip onto a backless stool without protest. I don't usually take orders—I give them. But something about this woman has me acting differently. Less murderous.

I could play it off as if I'm mellowing as I age, but that would be a copout. I wasn't mellow when I popped a bullet into a thug's head because he thought he could outsmart the Popovs' head hacker by doctoring the IP address of the company profiting from Miranda's metamorphosis. And I wasn't chill when I realized how many people had seen images of Miranda and me in varying arrays of undress.

For the most part, in the X-rated exposé, Miranda is covered. I was too up in her business to allow inches upon inches of her skin to be left without the attention of my hands, mouth, and cock, but the portions of her body you could see, and her expression when she orgasmed, turned my heart to stone.

I want to be the only man privileged to see them, and you can be certain I'll murder anyone who dares to look after me.

I'll track them down, every single one of the fools who have seen the footage, but I figured I should give the lady of the hour a heads-up on her recent surge in popularity before she finds out from someone other than her co-star.

"Help yourself," Miranda offers when she mistakes my moment of contemplation as desperation to sample one of the many baked goods on her kitchen counter. "There's more here than I could ever eat."

She mutters something under her breath, but I miss what she says. I can't hear a thing over the moan that rumbles up my chest when I pop a weird-looking rice bubble slice into my mouth. It tastes like heaven and sin—an equivalent of the flavors of its creator's pussy.

"That..." I stop talking, too busy stuffing another slice into my mouth to continue. "*Mm.*"

Miranda's grin makes my dick ache. "Ferrero Rocher slice"— she places down a similarly sized slice, but it is yellow instead of chocolatey brown and has shredded coconut on top—"is the perfect accompanier for a lemon coconut slice. The mix of sweet and sour and smooth and tarty is..."

She puckers her lips, and all I can think about is having them circling my cock.

I missed the chance when her confidence dipped to a point I couldn't ignore, but I'm not disappointed. Her pussy tastes godly, faultlessly matching her thoughts on her baked treats.

"... perfectly divine."

I don't even try to conceal my moan this time. The slices are delicious, and my taste buds dance with euphoria as much now as they did the afternoon she sat on my face.

A sense of achievement highlights Miranda's gorgeous

features as she cuts a piece out of all the baked goodies and places them onto a diabetic's-one-way-ticket-to-death charcuterie board.

She doesn't eat a single crumb. I want to say it is because she is full from sampling the goods while baking them like she did the whisky, but my top-of-the-class stalking skills announce that isn't true.

She's either holding back because she hates being eyeballed while eating, or she is a person who gets pleasure from watching others be pleased.

She didn't seem the latter when she lowered her pussy onto my face, but you can never tell.

I could smell how wet Tasha's pussy got while explaining to me how Miranda's severance of the camcorder cable wouldn't have removed the footage that had already been uploaded to her Only Fans page. And unlike the man I killed thirty minutes ago, the wet patch on the front of Miranda's husband's pants when she found him in the walk-in closet wasn't urine.

Roy pissed himself at the start of the proceedings. It smelled nothing like the rank smell that poured out of the closet when he wordlessly begged for Miranda's forgiveness like he wasn't surrounded by multiple pictures of his deceit.

Miranda's stomach grumbles again, drawing me from dangerous thoughts. It has grumbled multiple times over the past twenty minutes, sounding as ravenous as my mouth is to become reacquainted with her pussy.

I'm not the smartest man to ever be born, but it still kills me to admit it takes me three to four minutes to unearth why she's depriving herself of the items she slaved over for hours.

I almost backtracked on my pledge that I was satisfied with the outcome of my revenge plot when Roy couldn't hide his confusion for a second longer when I went to retrieve my gun.

He was of the same belief as everyone else in my realm—that a woman over a size two shouldn't be gawked at with admiration.

He thought a handful of negative and highly untrue comments about bigger ladies would have me running into the arms of the closest supermodel.

His lips didn't move an inch when I said I couldn't wait to take his wife for a second run.

I was stirring him. My life is way too complicated to throw someone as innocent as Miranda into the mess, but Roy didn't know that.

He arced up—stupidly.

I forced him to sit the fuck back down with both my fists and my words before I told him with utmost certainty that I wasn't playing when I warned him to stay away from Miranda. The instant she sat on my face, she was placed under my shelter. Anything done to her is done directly to me.

I'll kill a man for looking at me in the wrong manner, but it will be a lengthy death full of torture and deprivation if he dares to utter a bad word about Miranda under his breath.

Miranda's relaxed, calm composure shows how good Roy's absence the past three days has been for her, but it's done little to re-establish the confidence he eradicated from her on the daily before he filed for divorce.

And I'm done pretending it has.

"What do you say, *printsessa*? Lick for a lick and bite for a bite?"

7

MIRANDA

*N*ero removes his jacket before pushing back on the stool, placing a generous gap between the kitchen counter covered with slices, cakes, and cookies and him. There's an empty stool next to him, but his eyes gleam with so much need that even if I want to pretend the gap isn't for me, I can't.

Nero wears horny as obviously as I wear desperate.

I can smell it pluming from him.

That doesn't mean I'll act like a trollop, though.

I have class—*barely*.

"I—"

"I wasn't asking, *printsessa*. Get your fine ass over here. *Now.* I'm fucking starved."

I jump as if accustomed to taking orders, and Nero smirks as if he finds my submissiveness addictive.

My thighs quiver, either in excitement or worry, when he

lowers his eyes to my slinky pants. "If you want to keep your shirt, I'm fine with that, but you need to lose your pants." When I hesitate, he raises his eyes to my face, his gaze lingering on my breasts for two lazy, lust-filled seconds. "No one eats candy with the wrapper still on."

I angle my head and arch a brow, confused.

He said we were going to go bite for a bite, lick for a lick.

Why do I need to be naked for that?

I'm afraid the whisky-yuzu savarin will be dry when my smarts kick back on.

Nero doesn't want to go turn for turn on the treats I baked.

He wants to eat me.

The knowledge alone starts an inferno. For now, it is contained in my lower stomach. I don't see its containment lasting long.

Just standing across from him, panting and wet, I feel my temperature rising. My skin is scorching, and he hasn't even touched me yet.

I'm seconds from combusting.

Tremors race down my limbs when I hook my thumbs into the waistband of the pants I dug out of the back of my closet with purpose. Roy said the manufacturer was wrong for making them for people "my size" and that the only time I was permitted to wear them was when working out in the garage with the roller door closed.

I went grocery shopping in them this morning and didn't consider testing their elasticity before rummaging through the bottom of an industrial freezer, seeking my favorite flavor of ice cream.

My fupa could have been showing, and I couldn't have cared less.

I didn't endure a single scold, not now or this morning, and the remembrance is addictive.

"One minute." I hold my finger in the air to amplify my request before pivoting on my heel, the elastic in my pants snapping against my skin from the brisk removal of my hand.

Most women about to be devoured as if they're dessert would run to the bathroom to freshen up.

I bolt for the refrigerator.

I haven't had ice cream in years, and since the idea of being bitten down there scares me, I pick a meal that will require as many licks as it does nibbles to devour.

My nipples pebble against the thinness of my shirt when I return to Nero's half of the kitchen. His watch isn't icy. It's so searingly hot that any part not awarded the attention of his hooded gaze feels cold.

Nero moans when I place the tub of ice cream onto the section of the counter he cleared away before I stab my thumbs into the waistband of my pants. My ass jiggles and my breasts bounce when I pull the slinky material to my knees.

My fumble as I struggle to remove the rigid material is usually when I'd dive for the covers to hide my inflamed cheeks. Something stops me this time.

Or should I say, someone.

Nero watches me like I'm performing onstage. He's casually dressed in jeans, a white crew neck shirt, and black boots, but he is the essence of suave. He is a beautifully orgasm-inspiring man, and he knows it.

His smirk announces this, not to mention how he grabs his crotch to outline the massive bulge unconcealed by the zipper in his jeans when I finally get my pants to cooperate with my plan.

He's so cocky my confidence should falter in his presence.

It doesn't.

I want to be wanted *by him.*

Consumed *by him.*

Fucked *by him.*

I want *him* to remind me that beauty comes in all sizes, and that real men know this.

My pants are discarded at the side of the kitchen, halfway over Tempy's head. Her acrobatic routine to celebrate Nero's unexpected yet highly craved arrival exhausted her to the point she is sleeping with her tongue hanging out.

I step closer to Nero, trembling all over. A squeak pops from my lips when he lifts me to sit on the counter, and strain doesn't fetter his face. He positions me where he wants me without a single sign of discomfort shown, as if I am weightless.

Even when I was in my prime and at my ideal weight, I was never tossed around like a ragdoll.

I'm tall for a girl, which means the scales always tiptoed too close to what Roy classified as a "safe lift." That limited our activities to missionary, missionary, and you guessed it... missionary.

As Nero runs the back of his hand down the seam of my pussy, he raises his eyes to my face. He rolls his bottom lip between his teeth, pleased I forwent the small snippet of coverage my panties would have awarded me if I had left them on, but seemingly still disappointed.

I learn why when he says, "I know I said you could keep your shirt, but I'm gonna need to see your tits, *printsessa*. They feature heavily during my lengthy showering routines, and I don't want to miss the opportunity of adding another handful of mental snapshots to the vault load in my head."

As images of him stroking his cock over me squash my thighs together, I grip the hem of my shirt and whip it over my head.

My breasts fall heavily to my chest as air hisses from Nero's mouth.

I'm braless, and it seems as if he has only just noticed.

A tinge of shyness encroaches me when I realize I'm stark naked and he hasn't even undone the laces on his boots.

It shifts to greedy need when he takes no time reminding me that I'm the platter of his indulgence and that no man turns up to a buffet butt naked.

With the lid of the ice cream removed, and the soft, melted gooeyness on the rim edged by Nero's fat fingers, he raises his hand to my face.

Maple syrup and pecan flavors swamp my senses when he drags his index finger over my top lip before he slowly pushes it inside my mouth.

I moan as a burst of flavors ignite my taste buds, then growl when Nero returns the favor.

His mouth swamps my pussy like he knows the purpose of fat on a pubic bone before he drags his tongue up the lines of my pussy.

I'm tall for a girl, but my position on the counter and Nero's impressive height means he has no trouble commanding both my mouth and my pussy at the same time.

When he circles the nervy bud at the apex of my vagina, I

playfully nibble on the fingers he refilled with ice cream two seconds after he curls his tongue around my clit.

My ass nearly vaults off the counter when he makes true on his pledge to go bite for a bite. His teeth graze the hood of my clit before his tongue hits it with back-to-back flicks like I do to his fingers.

As tingles race across my stomach, I lick his fingers, my speed fast and unrelenting.

Nero matches my eagerness with as much attention to detail. He plunges his tongue inside my pussy before sliding it back to my clit, where he makes stars form with back-to-back licks.

"More," he demands when I lick and suck his fingers clean.

I'm so desperate to come I've eaten over half of the container of ice cream.

Almost absentmindedly, Nero shoves the small canister of French vanilla and pecan ice cream my way before he grips my meaty thighs, takes a seat on my stool, then drags me across the counter until my ass is suspended off the edge.

He eats me hungrily. *Desperately.* And I do the same to the ice cream.

I scoop it out of the tub without a spoon, hopeful the coolness of the frozen treat will simmer the fire raging inside me.

The wildfire in my stomach is burning out of control, and I moan as if the aftermath won't be catastrophic.

"*Mm,*" I moan when Nero licks up a droplet of the mess dribbling off my fingers and careening down my stomach. "Do that again."

"I'd rather eat you," he answers two seconds before he circles his tongue around my ice-cream-laden fingers, and he sucks down hard.

My thighs quiver as the fire in my stomach augments.

I'm seconds from combusting.

I think about the combined flavors of our desserts. It makes me so horny that before I can consider the possible outcome of my rampant need, I cup his bearded jaw and kiss him hard on the mouth.

We moan in sync, the mix of flavors more enticing than I could have ever imagined.

I'm not the only one who agrees.

Seconds after reloading his fingers with the ice cream, Nero stuffs them into my mouth.

I swallow down only half of the creamy goodness before his tongue scoops out the leftovers.

We go turn for turn until all the ice cream is gone and Nero has no choice but to return his head to between my legs.

He tongues my clit with controlled focus, driving me wild with need.

Rolling my hips, I grind against his mouth as he expertly eats me.

Pleasure skates across my skin as his name rips from my mouth.

When fireworks build, I try to hold back the urge, to savor my treat as if it's meant to be a rarity. But before I can fully swallow the desire to climax, the brilliance of our exchange overwhelms me.

I come with a hoarse cry, my body limp and pliable and my tremors as vocal as my moans.

Nero's drive doesn't waver in the slightest.

He toys with my clit while stuffing two fingers deep inside me, giving the walls of my vagina something to cling to as it rides the crazy wave threatening to pull me under.

His breath is hot and urgent against my drenched sex as he stretches my orgasm from one to two. He curls my toes with perfectly timed licks and mind-hazing furls of his fingers, and I am helpless to stop him.

I merely watch, enamored by his determined focus.

My head falls back as a rush of heated blood pulses around my body. I'm lost to the sensation, his unyielding attention too much for my body to bear.

I come again, the rush of euphoria shooting from the roots of my hair to the tips of my toes. My ears ring in the aftermath of my screams, and poor Tempy is startled. She's never heard such noises leave my mouth, and she has been my rescue dog for over half my married life.

Roy thought getting a dog would dampen my wish to become a mother.

It didn't, but that doesn't mean I love her any less.

Upon hearing the girlie laugh I can't hold back when Nero lifts me into his arms, Tempy licks her chapped mouth before she burrows her head into my pants and falls back asleep.

I'm so smitten by the ease of Nero's lift that I don't realize how intimately he knows the floor plan of my home until he maneuvers us out of the kitchen and through the living room before he climbs the stairs to the loft-like bedroom.

I'm about to ask him about it, when his trip on the toolkit I left out has his focus shifting from sampling every inch of my mouth to staring at the bed our once other halves used as an impromptu set for a porno.

Our lust bubble has been burst.

Or so I believe.

With his head slanted in a way that makes him appear more innocent than murderous, Nero asks, "Need help dismantling it?"

8

NERO

*W*hen Miranda wiggles as if my offer means I need to place her down, I shake my head before directing my steps to the bed responsible for the massive crinkle between her dark brows.

It doesn't affect me as it does Miranda. Why? I was married for four weeks. Three of those weeks I stayed at Clark's, the offsite compound of the Popov crew.

I tried to make my marriage work, but the odds were stacked against us more than a *Married at First Sight* contestant. Tasha and I have nothing in common. We are complete opposites, and although Tasha could see the signs as obviously as I could, she didn't want an annulment.

She wants a payday.

She may have gotten one—not a lot, but something is better than nothing—if she had left her side gig on the back burner for a few more weeks.

Only Fans is Tasha's bread and butter. She makes a decent living. As much as a runner, enforcer, and number three of one of the biggest crime syndicates in the world? Not fucking close. But I'm happy for her not to know that until after the divorce papers are signed.

If Tasha snoops, my ma will be brought into a fight she doesn't belong in. If that fight tells her I wed without her attendance *and* permission, my balls will be tacked to the wall in her condo not even thirty seconds later.

So, as much as I hate keeping secrets from my ma, I don't have a choice.

The storm will blow over relatively easily for me. Miranda won't be so lucky. From the defeat in her eyes when she stormed into the hotel room, and the date on the document I forced through the correct channels days earlier than necessary so her husband wouldn't die a martyr in his wife's eyes, I know her nuptials will take a little longer to get over.

I never anticipated I'd be one of the tools to help her forget him, but I'd be a liar if I said I wasn't grateful. Miranda is a great chick. She has fantastic tits, a ripe, salivating pussy, and enough gall not to be a doormat.

None of the women I've been with in the past twenty years have come close to the motivation Miranda hits my cock with any time I see her. She's more addictive than heroin, and I've only sampled the surface of her stimulants.

The reminder sees me tossing Miranda onto the mattress. Her giggles firm my cock more, but when I flip her over and drag her back... *fuck.*

Her ass is pure perfection.

It is too much for a boy to handle and has my plans jumping two steps ahead.

"Old girls like this need more than a ratchet to dismantle her."

Miranda stops wondering if my "old" reference is about her when I palm her dripping pussy before swiveling her clit between my index and middle fingers. We're the same age, but even if we weren't, nothing could derail this train. It is on the tracks, clattering toward climax station.

"The bolts seize from a lack of movement over *many* years."

Miranda moans with me when I curl my arm around her midsection and tug her back ruefully enough for the bed frame to screech in the process.

She isn't worried about us breaking her bed. She's concentrating on the firmness of my cock when it grinds against her ass, and how the bolts in the bed frame wouldn't be seized in place if they'd undertaken regular rocking sessions.

Tasha and Roy may have been photographed here and fooled around in this very bed, but they didn't fuck like thoroughbreds here.

The seized bolts tell a story Roy will never want shared.

I lower the hand groping Miranda's stomach as if its squishiness is as enticing as the fantastic swell of her tits—because it is—to the apex of her pussy.

My palm flattens against her clit as I rake two fingers between the folds of her wet cunt. She's still drenched, meaning I don't face an ounce of resistance when I stuff two fingers deep inside her.

She writhes, forcing her sexy thighs to shudder. The wish to beg is all over her face.

"Do you want to come again, *printsessa*? Are you greedy for more?"

When she remains quiet, I squash my palm down firmer, doubling the shudders of her panted breaths.

I don't want to catch her so I can pluck her wings like the vindictive fucks jealous of her reincarnation.

I just want a few more moments to admire her beauty before she flies away, never to be seen again.

Miranda's long glossy locks slip off her back and roll down her side when she peers back at me. She watches me under hooded lids for several seconds while I grind my cock against her ass and stimulate her pussy with my hand before she nods.

I smile like all my Christmases have come at once as I lower my hand to my jeans. Her watch when I unbutton my jeans and lower the zipper makes me painfully hard. She likes drinking in my body as much as I do hers.

Before I remove my cock from its tight restraints, I grip my shirt at the back of my neck and pull it over my head while toeing off my boots, my fingers never once moving from her slick canal. I finger fuck her with slow, purposeful pumps while stripping out of my clothes like she paid for the honor.

"You're so fucking wet," I murmur when the undeniable proof of her excitement glistens on my fingers. Her pussy tightens when I add, "You need to be. If you want the bolts to loosen enough you can add this piece of shit to the inferno keeping your neighbors' heating bill low over the past three days, you need to be taken hard and fast."

I thrust my hips forward, my cock's head skidding across the sensitive skin between her ass and her pussy.

Her ass cheek wobbles when I slap it, and its claps as I increase the speed of my pumps massage my cock when I rock it back and forth.

"Have you ever been fucked here?"

Her nonchalant headshake that announces she's never been taken hard and fast ever boosts when I swipe my thumb over a hole not gripping my fingers like she's seconds from release.

I groan. "Tempting. So fucking tempting. But if you want this bed gone, we'll have to save your ass's virginity for another time. I need to take you *hard*."

Will you listen to me, acting like this shouldn't be a one-time-only deal? Miranda's pussy tastes like heaven, and she is as dynamite as her body, but we're from very different worlds.

I distribute drugs.

She peddles sugary treats.

I'll kill a man for looking at me in the wrong manner.

She'd kill him with kindness even after he was a dick.

I'm hard, rough, and ready, and she's squishy and soft, making my dick fucking ache.

We're not the same, but my fucking god, it is impossible to think about anything but making her come when standing across from her. I like the way her doe eyes peer up at me without fear, how the thrusts of her chest become more urgent when our eyes lock, and the way not even being married for over a decade has her forgetting the name of the man bringing her to ecstasy.

I'm an addict and Miranda's pussy is my drug of choice.

Needing to get my head back into game mode, I slide my hips back and grip my length at the base. I'm not gripping it to thicken me more. I am strangling it into submission, wordlessly refusing its numerous pleas to give in to the sheer sexiness of the glistening on Miranda's thick thighs.

I could come now just from drinking in the way she's positioned in front of me.

I drop my forehead to her shoulder when she arches up, desperate to reacquaint our bodies. The change-up slicks the head of my cock with her wetness and drenches her clit with my pre-cum.

As I circle the base of my cock and jerk it to the rhythm of Miranda's hip thrusts, the engorged crown flicks the aching bud between her legs.

We dry hump until the wetness of our joined excitement is louder than our moans, and then I inch back until the head of my cock pierces the lines of her pussy.

"Please," she begs, her ass cheeks bouncing as she swivels her hips, welcoming me inside.

Just like the first time I took her, a pinch of pain hits my cock when I breach past her entrance. She's so fucking tight it takes everything I have not to blow my load once my cock's head has fully sunk inside her.

I take it slow for the first dozen pumps before the insane need to fuck claws at my chest, making me desperate.

I lunge forward fast, fully sinking in with one thrust.

Miranda doesn't seem to mind. Her screams bounce around the room as her begs for me to fuck her ramp up.

She pleads for me to take her hard and fast, to fuck her how she's never been fucked.

I oblige.

What red-blooded man wouldn't?

"Yes," I moan when she meets my thrusts grind for grind. "That's it. Take me. Accept my dick like a good little wifey."

Pleasure pulls my balls in close when she moans my name.

I fuck her lush, soft body with everything I have. I push her to the brink of insanity, on the crazy ride with me, until the headboard we're endeavoring to loosen bangs against the wall.

Its loud whacks announce the wildness of our embrace. The carnal animalistic fuck we're undertaking. It is the clap of the crowd knowing they're getting the performance of their lives, and it gives meaning as to why Tasha's subscribers doubled in less than thirty-six hours.

Miranda's body is a temple of seduction.

It was built to be fucked.

I love fucking her. And since it is a gift, not an expectation, I enjoy every minute she is willing to share with me. It isn't a chore like the women I used to get off with when my hand wasn't enough.

Her pleasure is my pleasure.

Miranda's pussy is so snug, amazingly firm around my cock, and wet. I pound into her without an ounce of resistance, only holding back to ensure the spasms her uterus faces are from the ebbs and flows of an incoming mind-hazing climax.

Her body quakes through my pounding thrusts, her knees skidding across the sheets, and her tits clapping from the force of my pumps.

I thrust harder.

"Take me."

Faster.

"All of me."

Rougher.

"Accept my cock like a good little wifey who can't get enough."

She comes with a cry, her pussy tightening around my throbbing shaft with the tightness of a fist.

"God," I grunt out, my voice husky with lust. "You're strangling my cock, begging it for its cum. You're going to make me come so hard."

I slap her ass, causing it to jiggle when her urge to drive me off a cliff sees her thrust back harder, fucking me as unrelentingly as I am fucking her.

She grinds her ass against me, taking me even deeper, before adding a teasing squeeze to every thrust.

I drive into her so fast the headboard no longer bangs against the wall. It bunny-hops away from it, the strength of my thrusts no match for the titanium-plated steel holding it together.

The bed's legs wobble as intensely as Miranda's thighs when she notices its sways. Her worry that the bed is about to fall into a heap beneath us doesn't weaken the intensity of our exchange, though.

We fuck wildly. *Crazily.*

We move in sync like we've been dancing this madly passionate tango for years.

Then, just as the mattress crashes to the floor, Miranda comes again.

"Fuck," I bite out, my balls throbbing as I try to stave off doing the same.

I lose the battle when Miranda shouts my name for the second time.

As I still my hips, I flare my nostrils, drinking in her scent, while my release pumps inside her in raring spurts.

9

MIRANDA

*S*weet lord, he did it.

He dismantled the bed I've been endeavoring to disassemble since I returned from the hotel.

I am too tired to add the frame to the fire I've kept stocked for the past three days, and the mattress to the charity collection pile.

I'm so zonked I could sleep for a week.

My eyes slowly flutter closed as I sink into the mattress I'll replace first thing tomorrow morning.

They don't remain shut for long. Nero's slow slip as he removes his still-firm cock from my pussy has my libido awakening as if I haven't orgasmed more times today than I have in the past three years.

The wetness coating his impressive manhood adds more slickness to the mess between my legs and heats my cheeks with more than lust.

We forgot to use protection. *Again.*

"I'm still on birth control." Nerves shudder my vocal cords. I hate the thought of him thinking I stayed on birth control because I plan to stay with my cheating husband.

My religious pill taking has nothing to do with Roy. My lust-craving heart was hopeful what we just did was a possibility. That maybe the flames our exchange combusted into in the hotel would one day reach my home base.

My head told my heart it was living in a fantasy world.

It'll be quick to apologize once it is at full function.

It will need more than a handful of wheezy breaths, though. My head is stuck in a fog it has no plans of escaping anytime in the next six to eight hours.

"Are you leaving?" I ask, hearing a ruffle, my voice still groggy.

A near-comatose state isn't to blame for my sluggishness. The fear of rejection means even something as simple as getting my eyes to follow the prompts of my brain takes almost ten seconds to initiate.

I don't want to watch Nero's departure. My psyche, though better than it was only days ago, is still a little fragile. It may break if it thinks I'm being rejected by the only man who has ever shown legitimate interest.

Relief washes over me when Nero replies, "No."

He continues for the open plantation shutters on the far side of the room. They face the road, but since we're on the second story and the house across the street is vacant, I don't bother closing them.

"But you should keep your blinds closed. You never know who may be looking in."

I wet my bone-dry mouth before cracking my lips for a smile.

"The house across the street has been vacant for almost a year. Roy said some rich schmuck bought it with the plan to flip it once the market improves."

Air whizzes from Nero's nose as he tugs the shutters shut, and then he slowly creeps back to the mattress now flopped on the floor.

I assume he is going to slip beneath the sticky sheets, so you can picture my surprise when he peels me off the material clinging to my skin and tosses me over his shoulder.

I'm naked, exhausted, and somewhat hungry, but I refuse to tell Nero that.

I've never been carried like I'm a damsel in distress or an up-and-coming mafia wife.

I'm also obsessed by the ease of his lift and the way it reminds me of my femininity. I grew up believing I'd be the caretaker of my home and that I'd blush every time I caught the admiring stare of my husband across the room. We'd make love against the railing of the water tower in my hometown after I was carried up its stairs without a bead of sweat dotting my husband's brow.

I never considered the only time I'd sweat after marriage would be while wrangling a lawn trimmer into submission, or from trying to burn off the calories I consume in excess, because I eat when depressed, on rusty gym equipment in the garage of a home not in my name.

My life turned out nothing like I had planned, and only last week, I thought I was too old to change it.

How stupid have I been? Thirty-five isn't close to ancient. I've not even lived half my life yet, and I refuse to waste another second on things that don't matter.

With my mood suddenly perky, I don't attempt to cover myself when Nero places me onto the vanity so he can switch on the shower.

My shower stall is one of those annoying, fully enclosed glass boxes that restrict movements. I hit my elbows while washing my hair, so although I admire Nero's un-voiced suggestion that we wash the stickiness off our skin together, it isn't practical.

I'll wait on the vanity, enjoying the show while pondering how little I know about the man standing before me as naked as the day he was born.

It isn't a hard feat. Nero is as striking out of his clothes as he is in them. Muscles upon muscles, lines and lines of ink, and a huge cock that never seems to deflate.

He is insanely attractive, and I'm more than happy to waste hours sampling everything he has to offer—both inside and out of the package.

"What do you do for a living?" Nero checks the temperature of the water pumping out of the faucet before twisting to face me. His nose is crinkled, and his brows are furled, but there's a touch of playfulness in his eyes that frees me to say, "I'm assuming bounding and gagging your cheating spouse's conquests and stuffing them in a closet is a side gig, so what do you do the rest of the time to earn a living?"

Reminding him that he was cheated on probably isn't a smart move. It could prompt him to the fact that we're more a rebound than anything, but since I need to be reminded of that as well, I run with it.

There's a moment of tension, then a trickle of humor. "It is presumptuous to assume there isn't a ton of money in defiling the cheaters of the world, butterfly."

Butterfly?

He continues talking, moving my contemplation of my nickname to a later date. "Numerous TV shows on that very subject have brought in millions of viewers and just as much capital."

Since everything he says is true, I don't disagree with him.

"I was once one of them," I admit.

"Once?"

It is almost impossible to keep my eyes on his face, but I must. His tone gives nothing away, so if I don't drink in his numerous expressions, I will have no clue if he's angry or relaxed.

At the moment, he's calm enough for me to say, "I saw a few too many similarities between the cheaters' excuses and the ones Roy gave me anytime he was out late or didn't come home at all."

Now he's somewhat peeved. "So Tasha wasn't the first woman he cheated on you with?"

I shake my head before switching it for a shrug. "I don't have any proof, but I'm reasonably sure she is one of many."

Nero takes a moment to contemplate before he plucks me from the vanity like my shower is double its size. He drags us under the spray while muttering, "Shows how much of a fucking tool your soon-to-be ex is."

Shockingly, we fit. There isn't enough room for a snippet of air to be placed between us, but I'm not bothered. Our conversation is more cleansing than any shower could be.

"So the teddy... *that fucking teddy*"—his growl sets me on fire —"was that payback? Or for someone else?"

I groan, wishing I could be as vindictive as a perpetrator

when done wrong, but aware I would have never gone through with what we did if I hadn't been handed divorce papers beforehand.

Two wrongs won't make a right.

"It was more... *desperation* than anything?" Since I am unsure of my reply, it sounds like a question instead of a confirmation. "Roy had promised to try, and our vows said for better or worse, so I was trying to drill through the worse." When Nero's expression switches from lusty to sympathetic, I alter the direction of our conversation. "But that's enough about me. How about we go back to if you're looking at filming a remake of *Cheaters* or keeping it as a side gig until something better comes along."

He smiles, loving the playfulness in my tone, before he says, "Depends on how well Roy behaves."

I swallow the brick his reply lodged in my throat but remain quiet.

He didn't rough Roy up a little like previous participants of the *Cheaters* show. He bruised him, nicked him, and scoured a derogative word into his forehead.

He also admitted he had intended to kill him before I arrived.

The remembrance should make the shower water chilly.

It doesn't, and I am at a loss as to why.

I've never believed violence is the solution, but my thoughts changed when I read the divorce paperwork Roy forwarded the day of our wedding anniversary.

Roy went for blood, so it is logical that I fight back just as dirtily.

Do I wish he were dead? No.

But I'm not opposed to a bit of help if it plays the player at his own game.

"He wants the house." I don't snarl until I finalize my statement. "And Tempy."

Nero hits the nail on the head. "Because he knows they're the two things that will hurt you the most to lose." He stares straight into my eyes while revealing his insides aren't as hard as his outsides. "He's a drop of salty water in the ocean. But this"—his eyes flick around my bathroom—"is your home, and Tempy is your baby."

"A baby with a bite bigger than her bark."

He laughs like he knows I'm not lying. I guess he can. Tempy bit Roy so hard during our last argument that she left a scar. It is on his left thigh, right near the area I had tattooed months ago.

I still as excitement blisters through me.

Is that why Nero called me butterfly? Because of my tattoo? I got it in rebellion, but a part of me, a side I've kept well hidden, was hoping that one day it would reflect my transformation from Roy Martin's wife to Miranda Richardson, entrepreneur and *Forbes* Woman of the Year.

The last item on my wish list is a stretch, but if you don't believe in yourself, how can you believe in anyone else? We will back hair-raising ideas from celebrities but turn our nose up at an idea from a family member or friend.

I truly don't get it. Support should come from those closest to you, not strangers.

Though I'd rather not remember that right now.

Nero is a stranger, yet he's supporting me through what is

meant to be the hardest time in my life that seems more easy than concerning.

Desperate to return his support, I ask, "Have you filed?"

A hum sounds from his chest before he directs me under the spray.

Once my locks are drenched from the roots to the tips, he adds words to his reply. "A couple of weeks back. I originally filed for an annulment. When Tasha refused to sign, I switched it to a divorce."

His honesty is refreshing, but it doesn't hide the truth.

"So, technically, Tasha wasn't cheating." I speak slowly, unsure if this is the direction I should take.

I don't want to defend what Tasha did, but I'm willing to give her a little leeway if it keeps my guilt at bay.

I fucked a stranger an hour after being handed divorce papers.

Tasha may have waited weeks.

"Technically... I guess you are right." He sounds confused, and it has me wanting to push on the brakes, but I lose the chance when he adds, "But I feel like there's more to her story than she's sharing, so I have the right to be apprehensive."

"You do," I agree. Needing to ease the tension, I playfully barge him. "Just like I have the right to tell you not to be such a hog."

I'm an inferno in an instant when he replies, "Are you talking about the water? Because if you're not, and you are more hinting about your sinfully delicious and tight cunt, I have *every* right to be a hog."

Cunt is such a crude word, but it sounds sensual in his native twang. It rolls through me like liquid ecstasy and has me wishing my shower stall wasn't such a confined space.

"We had an agreement, butterfly. Bite for a bite." He playfully bites my lips, sending my head into a tailspin. "Lick for a lick." My thighs squeeze when he drags his tongue along the seam of my mouth, tasting me. "So it is only fair that I get to wholly fucking devour you after your cunt"—he says the word like he knows my thoughts on it—"swallowed my dick like it was created *for me.*"

His last two words are my undoing. I want him. Again. Now. Any way I can get him.

And I need only one word to have him. "Please."

10

NERO

"*N*ero!"

Miranda's amazing tits bounce as I drive into her hard. Her thighs glisten with as much sweat as evidence of her multiple arousals as her ankles lock around my lower back, endeavoring to slow my pounds.

I don't give in. I fuck her hard and impatiently, needing to ensure not an ounce of the shame she felt last night while pondering the comments our X-rated video may have attracted will trickle through her veins when we go our separate ways this morning.

None of the comments I saw were bad. I would have driven straight to the commenter's house and ripped their eyes out of their sockets if they were negative. But a woman with a beaten ego needs more than a worded confirmation.

She needs to feel desired and be desired.

She needs to be fucked with a hunger only a man wanting to place his woman on a pedestal can instigate.

Last night, both in the shower and on the floor next to the bed we destroyed, we explored with a tenderness I've never held an interest in but will now crave.

This morning's romp is on the other end of the spectrum.

I'm driving her to the brink of insanity one impatient yet calculated pump at a time.

And Miranda can't get enough.

She claws at my back and screams my name as her tight cunt ripples around my unsheathed shaft. She feels so fucking good, bare and slick.

The need to come is clawing at me, thrumming through my veins as rampantly as Miranda's taste flooded my tongue when I woke her by consuming her pussy for breakfast.

I spread her wide with my shoulders before I parted a pussy that tastes as sweet as honey with my fingers.

Pre-cum leaked from my cock when I marveled at the feast in front of me.

I toyed with her clit until the word I was desperately seeking slipped from her O-formed mouth.

"Please."

Then I went to town on her pussy. I rubbed at her clit with my thumb while I pushed my tongue deep inside her.

Her pussy quivered around my tongue as it does my cock now when she's swamped by a blinding orgasm for the second time this morning.

The pressure of her tight squeezes on my cock is exquisite. I want to come, to follow her down the blistering side alley of sex and euphoria, but I hold back the urge, needing more.

More tension.

More connection.

More *her.*

My butterfly is soaring so high that her wings will never be clipped, but I can't let go just yet. There's still so much to do, so many mistakes to right, and at least a dozen more orgasms she was depraved of by a weasel with a corn kernel for a cock.

Miranda's body tenses as her back arches. Her climax is draining but also giving. It sparks fresh hope in her eyes and clears away the last smidge of unease hours of foreplay, touching, and fucking couldn't remove.

We didn't solely spend our night twisted beneath sheets. We also talked. I kept my replies basic, not wanting to scare her, but she knows that I'm in distribution and entertainment. She's just unaware that I distribute drugs across the globe and that most entertainment in Vegas includes strippers and prostitutes.

In all honesty, I don't think she will be bothered, but Nikolai's business plan isn't mine to share. I'm paid a hefty sum to assist in the running of his multiple billion-dollar businesses, and I would rather be a dead man than a tattler.

When Miranda returns from the clouds of lust her climax surged her to, I thrust hard, putting my weight behind my pumps.

As her pussy ripples around me, she moans my name again while signs of an imminent orgasm resurface.

"Fuck, *printsessa.* You're going to make up for those years of a dry spell in days at this rate."

I cuss again, inwardly this time, frustrated that she makes me so unhinged that I'm unknowingly sharing guarded secrets.

It was the same last night. Usually, I shut down any "get to know me" conversations within seconds of them jumping from the gate. I struggle doing that with Miranda. I want her to know me. The *real* me.

And the proof is undeniable when I say, "Take me. Let me in. I want you to feel me every time you shift an inch today."

The worried expression on her face softens before she does as asked. The already generous sweep of her thighs widens more as the movements of my hips slow. We're still fucking, *desperately*, but it isn't the dirty, hard romp I instigated when I woke her. It is more intimate, with a lot of eye contact and hungry, yearn-filled kisses.

I break our embrace when a vise-like grip pulls my balls in close to my body before I reach down between us.

Miranda's breaths are as hot as the slickness coating my shaft when I roll her clit with my thumb. Her nails claw at the sheets before she bundles them into her palm.

"You're so deep."

The need in her voice and the way she looks up at me while I pound into her are my undoing.

An endless moan pours out of me as beads of cum shoot from my cock.

Miranda joins me.

She writhes against me, open and defenseless as the annoying bellow of an alarm clock shrieks from her purse dumped in the corner of the room.

"I'm so sorry." As Miranda moves around her home, gathering her things, she continues offering up apologies I don't deserve. "I hate to eat and run, but this client has done amazing things for the creative side of my business, and I really don't want to disappoint her."

Her smile at the start of her sentence ensures I know she isn't mentioning the food we shared yesterday.

She's talking about when she was on her knees, inside the shower, swallowing my cock like she was born to do it.

"Are you sure you're okay to wait with her?" Her eyes stray to Tempy like she knows she won't need to see my reply to understand it. "She usually goes potty straight after breakfast. Then she will be out cold for the rest of the day."

I wait for her to gather her keys and spin to face me, before replying, "We'll be fine. Go."

Her sexy fucked-to-within-an-inch-of-their-life eyes lower to my mouth for the quickest second before she awkwardly waves. After patting Tempy's head while whispering that she will be home soon, she heads for the exit.

I'd be disappointed about no goodbye kiss if I were a man who did lovey-dovey shit. I'll give a compliment when a compliment is due, like last night when the head of my cock tickled Miranda's tonsils, but the fawning, lovemaking, and I-love-yous after one date do my head in.

I much prefer the look on Miranda's face when she stumbles out the door, her strides almost bowlegged. And how the defeated, sad look her eyes have rarely been without the past several months has all but vanished. I like the snippet of pain that hardens her features when she slips into the driver's seat of her car, and how it shifts to lust in half a nanosecond.

And I really like the way her nostrils burst when she smells me on her skin.

Her happiness means there's no one for me to bury today.

Will I feel the same when I work through the issues that have been bugging me since last night? Probably not. But the fact I've held back for so long shows growth.

I watch Miranda reverse out of her driveway and drive away, before twisting to face Tempy. She has devoured the funky-smelling breakfast Miranda placed out for her before she ran around her kitchen, bundling up the baked goods she made yesterday for me to take with me. She's finished and looks on the cusp of exhaustion.

"Potty first," I demand, my words cracking out of my mouth like a whip. "Then you can sleep."

Miranda and I won't be so lucky. I've got a shit ton of work to do before I arrive at Clark's, and Miranda's schedule exposes her calendar is just as brimming.

I smirk at Tempy when she does her business on the singed remains of Roy's belongings.

With a possessive scratch on the manicured lawn, she prances away like even her shit is too good for him, matching my sentiments to a T.

Dogs know good people.

Roy isn't one of them.

"Upstairs or downstairs?" I ask after recalling Miranda's announcement that Tempy's age means she can't climb the stairs, but that it hasn't stopped her love of the sunshine that streams through the doors of the upstairs balcony.

I scoop Tempy into my arms and begin climbing the stairs when she yaps and twirls, confident she'll tear my nuts off if I've mistaken her answer.

She licks my face during the climb, stealing some of Miranda's scent, before leaping out of my arms. She lands on a doggie daybed on the edge of the balcony.

"You good?" I ask when she circles the fluffy white micro mattress for almost thirty seconds, searching for the perfect spot.

I scratch her ear when she barks before she snuggles in deep, and then I leave as promised.

My trip "home" doesn't take long. In eight lengthy strides, I exit Miranda's property and enter the front door of my current abode.

I hear Eight in the kitchen, helping himself to the minimal supplies I had delivered last week, but I don't stop to greet him. I head straight to the basement with one thing on my mind, and one thing only.

A snivel hits my ears when I enter the damp confines. The basement hasn't been converted, so unlike the seemingly springish day outside, it is cold and damp, the perfect flu aggravator.

A cold isn't the cause of the sniveling, though.

It is the whine of a man in fear for his life.

Good.

He's only alive because I still have a use for him.

I drag over a chair, the wooden legs sawing like the strenuous effort of the lungs of the man watching my every move. His left eye is almost swollen shut, his lips are cracked and bleeding, and the stains on his pants have me grateful I've not yet had the floors done.

Piss is impossible to get out of pricy wooden floorboards.

Blood is much easier.

With one of the chair's legs balancing on two exposed toes, I take a seat.

The man bound to a rickety chair cries out, his eyes bulging as his long toe and middle toe collapse under the brunt of my weight.

His sobs make him incoherent. Since I need to hear his pathetic excuse in person, I pull out the bloody handkerchief I stuffed into his mouth before leaning in close.

I'm an inch from his bloodied and bruised face when I ask, "What is this I hear about you wanting her house *and* her dog?"

11

MIRANDA

*S*hiloh, my business partner, who isn't actually my business partner since she refuses to accept the title, slips into my car before fighting past her crazy curls to grab the seat belt latch.

"I was starting to think you weren't coming. You are usually half an hour early..." She stops talking with the silver part of the belt suspended in midair.

I start to panic that I wear harlot well when she slings her eyes to me so fast that I'm certain she'll be out of commission for a month with whiplash.

She doesn't speak. She just stares, her gawk a cross between admiration and disgust.

The cause of her alarm dawns when she murmurs, "It worked."

Since she isn't asking a question, more summarizing, I remain quiet.

"The teddy worked."

She looks like she wants to vomit. Since it is a rare expression for her to wear, I double the urge by waggling my brows.

Shiloh pushes past the carrot I'm dangling in front of her, going straight for the juicy slice of cake our out-of-town meetings usually inspire.

Roy has me on a banned list at all bakeries and cafes within fifteen miles of our home.

"Nope. No. I refuse to believe it." She finishes latching her belt so I can begin our trip to our latest client's chosen wedding location. "I've known Roy for as long as I've known your sexy ass. He doesn't have *this*"—she wiggles her perfectly polished nails in my face—"in him." I roll my eyes when she says, "Where the hell has my I-haven't-climaxed-in-my-entire-adult-life boss gone? This hussy ain't her."

She sniffs me, doubling the heat of the stare of the person stopped at the traffic light next to us. He looks as desperate to take a bite out of Shiloh's booty as Nero was mine last night.

"How many times did you orgasm over the weekend? From the sweat slicking your skin, I'd say over half a dozen." She tsks, her head cracking side to side. "So I stand by my statement. Roy does not have *this* in him."

I hold on for as long as I can before breaking the news, and then I try to take the non-adulterous route.

"Roy filed for divorce on day zero of the four-day anniversary-moon vacation I forced him to take so we could spend some quality time together."

Shiloh scoffs, but that's the beginning and end of her reply.

"It was couriered to me while he was in a honeymoon suite... with his mistress."

She's practically panting, dying for me to continue.

Since I am just as desperate to move through my shock of the past few days, I continue.

"While wearing the teddy you mentioned earlier, I went to the hotel to confront him."

If she gets up in my business any more, she'll be sitting on my lap. That's how close she sits to make sure she doesn't miss a word I speak.

"Roy wasn't the only person in the room when I let myself in."

My silence leaves Shiloh no option but to interrupt. "Someone was there with him?" When I nod, her mouth falls open. "His mistress?"

"No," I answer a little too loudly. I startle the commuter next to us as much as the person behind him does when they beep, announcing to him the light has switched to green. I shift to first while saying, "It was the husband of his mistress."

That sounds bad even to me, but Shiloh acts oblivious. "Holy shit cakes. So the people who were being cheated on cheated with each other?"

I hate the way she makes it sound, but there's no denying the truth.

I nod, and again, Shiloh's mouth falls open. "What did he look like? Was he hot? Did he have tattoos? Did he do nasty shit to you? Was he everything Roy will *never* be?"

My nods are endless, and they feel as freeing as Nero's attention has made me.

"He was..." I bite my bottom lip, and Shiloh goes crazy. She rocks her hips and makes inappropriate noises like I wasn't married the last time we spoke.

"Miranda!" She looks like she wants to pinch my cheeks like my aunts did in my youth. "I'm so fucking happy for you. This is exactly what you need."

"It's not like that," I say, shifting gears. I bought a stick shift car on purpose. It means Roy can never borrow it. He can't multitask, so steering and changing gears is above his skill set. "It was just an *at the time* type of thing."

Shiloh sinks into her seat, her exhale a harrumph.

She only stays down for half a second. "Then why do you smell like a hot hunk of a man now? Your anniversary was *four* days ago." Her tongue slithers like Hannibal. "I can practically taste the testosterone slicking your skin. If this god, who finally showed you what you're worth, used protection, he must have marked his territory all over you with the remnants left in the bottom of the condom and you refused to shower."

"You're disturbing," I say with a laugh, stupidly nervous.

"And straight up fucking honest. The hotter your cheeks become, the more cum I smell." An inane amount of jealousy smacks into me when she breathes in deeply and then releases it with a moan. "It is too fresh to act like it was from days ago."

"Because it isn't," I admit, talking slowly. "He came over last night." She pants like a dog in heat, impatiently waiting. "And should be gone by now since Tempy—"

"He stayed to watch Tempy?"

"No... he... ah... He said he would wait for her to finish breakfast and then take her outside to go potty before locking up for me." That couldn't sound more domestic if I had planned it. "I was running late. We... ran a little over on an activity this morning, so I..." I give in. "So he agreed to watch Tempy for me until it was her naptime."

Shiloh squeals. "He spent the night *and* watched your baby! Are you sure you're not already married?"

I wish divorce litigation worked that fast. "He stayed because he had something important to tell me, and I delayed the process because he likes feeding me as much as he loves eating me."

Where the hell did that hussy come from? I should be fuming mad that my naked derriere was uploaded to the world wide web. Or at the least, panicked. But Nero's attention has made my confidence so high unwanted attention a video like that could stir up doesn't seem as taunting as it once did.

Shiloh stares at me with her mouth hanging open and her eyes bulging. "He likes to... *eat*..." She lowers her eyes to my crotch hidden by a momma pouch I have no right to have. "Down there?"

I've not kept a single thing from her in the five years we've worked together, so I won't now.

I nod, my cheeks turning the color of beets.

"And he loves feeding you?"

The heat turns excruciating as I recall our time in my kitchen. The oven was on, but it wasn't the reason the cookies were as hard as rocks this morning. They were meant to be cooling, not facing an extensive re-bake.

It takes Shiloh just as long to remember I am married as it did me this morning when I contemplated kissing Nero goodbye.

Rebound fucks don't kiss each other goodbye, but it took me

longer than I care to admit to work that out only thirty minutes ago.

"And where was Roy during this... *foray*?"

"Um..." I pause, swallow, then try again. "The first time, he was in the closet."

She slaps my arm in shock so firmly that I veer into oncoming traffic.

I've only just righted the van, saving our lives, when she asks, "The closet of the hotel where you did the nasty with his mistress's husband?"

I nod, words above me.

"It could have been worse," I stammer out when her silence has me desperate for noise. "I could have arrived after Nero had finished what he went there to start."

To shock someone like Shiloh into silence is scary.

I've never seen her so quiet.

"Nero?" she says a short time later, her throat working hard to swallow.

The hair I pulled back in a hurry bobs when I nod.

Her brow is as piqued as her interests. "What hotel did you say it was, again?"

"I didn't." My voice is rife with suspicion. Shiloh looks like she's seen a ghost. That only happens when she has.

"It wasn't on Westward Boulevard, was it?"

Time slows to a snail's pace when I slowly jerk up my chin. "Have you heard of it before? It is relatively new."

Her nod is slow. It is as timed as the words she speaks next. "It is owned by the groom-to-be we're about to cater for, and everyone this side of the country knows his business partner on that particular project, and many others around Vegas, is named Nero." She sinks low in her seat, her confusion picking up. "So did you mix pleasure with business, or did Nero take the pleasure out of his business?"

"What do you mean?" I ask, too confused to try to work through my bewilderment alone.

Shiloh waits a beat before saying, "That hotel, and numerous others on the strip, *cater* for a certain clientele."

I nod, recalling the guest in the elevator who mistakenly believed I was a hooker.

"The hotel is co-owned by a man named Nero." The pieces are slowly slotting into place, so Shiloh whacks them in with a hammer. "So why would Nero's wife pick that hotel out of all the hotels in Vegas to get naughty with another man?"

That's a good question, and one I don't know how to answer.

Mercifully, Shiloh isn't quiet when she is confused.

She works through her uncertainty out loud.

"She'd have to have a death wish... or she wanted Nero to find out. Those are the only two plausible explanations." Her words slow as her brows pull together. "Unless..." Worry crosses her cutesy features, hardening them. "When did you say Roy filed, again? Date *and* time?"

"Friday afternoon around five. Why?"

She looks like she wants to slice Roy's balls off, and I'm right there with her when she says, "Close of business for all banks, insurance agencies, and superannuation funds."

This time, I veer into oncoming traffic on purpose.

12

NERO

Smoke filters into the basement. It isn't from Eight. That fucker knows my thoughts on the toxins passive smokers face. Also, his drug of choice is more lethal than nicotine, and ten times more fun.

"What the fuck did you do now?" I ask when the cell phone on the table next to me vibrates.

I recognize the number flashing across the screen of Roy's phone. The face that arrives with the number is unrecognizable, though.

The sad, beaten-down woman snapped by a man who rates beauty by clothing sizes isn't close to the image that pops up in my head when Miranda enters my thoughts.

She's beautiful and beaming with life in my flashbacks. She looks like she has nothing to live for in the picture Roy selected to store her number under.

With the blade of my knife, I signal for Roy to remain quiet before I slide my thumb across his phone's screen, answering Miranda's call.

"You fucking piece of shit," she snaps out a second after our call is connected. "Everything I worked for, my house, my business, my baby, you put in your mistress's name. Why would you do that, Roy? Why would you take everything *I* have worked for and give it to her?"

Her sniffle as she fights to hold back a sob pisses me off. It also makes me conscious as to why I brought my knife to the basement when I arrived home and has me itching like fuck to use it.

Roy's balls aren't big enough to hang off the back of my truck and be noticeable, but they'll make a nice rearview mirror ornament for Miranda. She can whack them every time she's pissed off, which is more often than her lungs have sucked in air in the past four days.

"I would have given you half. You didn't deserve *any* of it, but I still would have given you half because that's the right thing to do when you've been married for fourteen years." She stops to breathe through her anger and then comes back stronger than ever. "But now... now you won't get a single fucking cent. *You* cheated, Roy. *You* broke the vows of our marriage. So now *you* will suffer the consequences of *your* betrayal."

Miranda's scream echoes when it sounds down the line *and* through the thin walls of my basement. It prompts Roy to the location of his torture chamber and makes him as panicked as fuck.

His nostrils flare when he recalls how I comforted his wife the last time he fucked her over, and the salt it inspires rubs in deep when a second after Miranda ends her call with him, her name pops up on my phone's screen.

I admire the photo I snapped of her unawares before answering her call. "Hey..."

Even if I hadn't overheard her one-sided confrontation with Roy, I'd still be able to tell she is upset. Her voice is croaky, and her breaths are coming out fast.

"What's wrong, butterfly?"

Roy sneers at me, assuming I'm acting worried for a direct route into his wife's panties.

I backhand him across the face, *hard*, just for the insinuation.

I've watched Miranda from afar for almost a year, so you can be assured this isn't the first time I've asked her those exact words.

It is merely the first time I've said them loud enough for her to hear.

"I... ah... I just..." I've been used for years, so her struggle to ask for help isn't unexpected. Her next words, though, sure are. "I think your wife wanted you to find out about the affair."

I keep my voice calm and collected even though I am anything but. "Why do you say that?"

"It's just... um..."

She doesn't want to hurt my feelings, and it makes me like her a little bit more.

"Nothing you can say will shock me, butterfly."

You shouldn't be able to hear a smile, but I can.

It radiates down the line and makes my cock throb.

"I just have a weird feeling she wanted you to find out about the affair, so I thought I should share it with you. You said you were wary of her intentions, so perhaps it centers around this?"

"Perhaps," I echo. "It would make sense as to why they chose that location. You'd have to be pretty airy to check in at your spouse's hotel and expect him not to find out."

Miranda breathes a sigh of relief, and I smile like a smug prick.

I've only officially been in her life for days, yet she still cares about me more than she cares for the fool seated in front of me with piss-stained pants and a battered face. Her sigh announces this, not to mention her next words. "I should let you go. You're probably busy. I just wanted to warn you about any possible backlash that may be heading your way."

"I appreciate the heads-up."

If my reputation is anything of importance to me, I should leave it there.

Since it isn't, I continue.

"I'll also never be too busy for you, butterfly." I clamp my hand over Roy's mouth before rocking in my seat, crunching his broken toes on the dirty floor when he dares to sneer at me. "I was just about to take a break. You're more than welcome to keep me company."

Roy's pained breaths stop beading condensation on my palm when I gesture for him to be quiet again before I move to a laptop set up in the corner of the basement.

As he breathes though his nose, his throat too hoarse to uphold my silent warning of retribution, I flick through multiple live surveillance feeds until I find Miranda.

The smoke lingering in the air makes sense when I spot her

near a raging fire pit. One of the legs of the bed we broke last night is halfway burned. She has a second leg in her hand, ready to scorch it, but my offer sees her placing it onto the lawn next to a deckchair.

Her action shows she is accepting my offer, but her words say the opposite. "I'm not sure I'll be the best company."

"Because?" I ask, shocked.

I usually bolt for the hills before encouraging a conversation. I don't want to do that this time around. If she's willing to share the cause of the heavy groove between her brows, I'm willing to listen.

"It's just... stuff I don't want to bore you with."

"Then why don't we talk about stuff that won't bore me?"

I hit Roy with a stern finger point, cautioning him to remain quiet when my next question riles him enough to tighten his jaw. I didn't think he had it in him to go against me two times in a row. I'll be sure not to make the same mistake twice once I've finished calming his wife.

"Like what are you wearing right now?"

I don't mean to make things sexual between us twenty-four-seven, but tell me one woman who would lack confidence knowing they can make a man as hard as steel by doing nothing but breathing.

My dick leaks pre-cum just at the thought of Miranda's smile, but words have little effect on a woman who has had them used against her time and time again, so I'd rather show her.

Actions will always speak louder than words, and my logic couldn't be closer to the truth when Miranda laughs. Her giggles send a current straight to my dick and have my stomach grumbling like I didn't burn through half her treats in under six hours.

"I'm wearing what I had on when I waved goodbye to you this morning."

"Ah, yes. I remember. That sexy little red skirt with a flirty see-through blouse." Her somewhat conscious laugh switches to genuine when I add, "Exactly who were you meeting with, again, and at what location?"

Since she is unaware I know all the details of her meeting and the couple she met with, she tries to subdue my implied jealousy in a noncontroversial way. "I work mostly with couples madly in love."

Her swallow is audible when I reply, "As do I." I rarely speak business with anyone not in the business, but the ease of our interaction has me more open than I usually am. "But rarely do they enter my hotels together."

I watch her fight with herself for almost a minute before she asks, "Does that bother you?"

"No," I answer honestly. "Because if they're gonna cheat, they're gonna cheat. There's nothing we can do to stop them."

Only now do I realize she partially blames herself for Roy's inability to keep his dick in his pants. I can't say I don't understand. He beat down her confidence so much over the past fourteen years that anything that requires judgment has her immediately looking in the mirror.

It dawns on me that part of her contemplation was for me when she says, "I just don't get it. Roy cheated because Tasha is—"

"Shallow, opinionated, and so far up her own ass her breath smells like shit?"

Miranda's confidence flourishes on her face and in her voice. "She is also beautiful... and tiny. To some men, that's all they need." Before I can remind her that size has nothing to do with beauty, she says, "But what is Tasha's excuse? Roy is..." Her sigh hurts her soon-to-be ex more than my fists ever could. "He was nice once, but no amount of sheen can hide rotten insides for long. I should have left him years ago."

"That's why men like him get their butterflies before they've cocooned. Young and optimistic allows them to be weighed down before they learn the full strength of their wings." The reason behind my nickname comes to light when I say, "That's why you've got to play him at his own game, butterfly. Show him that you can fly even while your wings are damaged."

"I don't know if I can," she whispers, her voice defeated. "He took everything."

"Everything?" I ask, my glare hot enough to burn as I shift my eyes back to the vermin siphoning the blood from his wife's veins while she's still breathing.

I mouth to Roy that I'm going to kill him when Miranda answers, "All my equipment, my catering van. He even sold the ovens we use for catering events like the one I am meant to host this weekend. I have nothing to serve on, so even if I could get suppliers to deliver stock to me on the bad credit I now apparently have, I can't offer my clients the level of service I promised. It's over. I have to cancel all my upcoming events, including your business partner's upcoming nuptials."

There's no fear in her voice. No disgust. She knows my warts and doesn't care about them, which frees me to say, "Did you forget what industry I'm in? I can get you anything you need in less than twenty-four hours. There's no need to cancel anything."

Miranda proves she is as smart as she is beautiful, and it triples my obsession faster than I can click my fingers. "The white powder I'm seeking is a little different from what you usually distribute, Nero."

I thought the depth of my involvement in the Russian mafia syndicate making me rich would have her running scared. I should have known better.

It is easy to soar when you give up everything weighing you down.

I don't bother continuing to hide who I am. Miranda has seen me at my worst, rampant on vengeance and cloaked with danger, so she can see the real me as well. Her unexpected but highly craved respect has earned the honor.

"If it wasn't, would you accept it? Would you let a man like me help you?"

She contemplates for barely a moment before answering with a dignity she will never be without if I have it my way. "Yes... for a fair finder's fee."

My smile is heard in my words. "Then send me a list so we can skip to swapping services with no funds exchanging hands."

I don't need to be paid a finder's fee. I've already found her. She's mine. No fee needed.

"Nero—"

"Send me a list," I repeat, not needing her gratitude, but confident that is what she wants to give. "I'll get everything you need, and then some."

"Some?"

I let silence speak on my behalf.

Tiny panting breaths have never been more vocal.

"Okay." Miranda wrangles with her emotions for ten seconds before she blurts out, "I'll give you a list tonight when you come over."

"I'm coming over?" When she looks worried, like she didn't hear my thoughts as accurately as she did, I say, "I'll see you at eight," before I disconnect our call.

After dumping my phone onto the table holding my laptop, I reacquaint my fist with Roy's face.

The brutal collision dots my shirt with blood, meaning I will need to change again before visiting my favorite neighbor, but the crunch of his nose and the split of its bridge makes the sacrifice worthwhile.

I knew I kept this fucker alive for a reason. I just had no clue it would be for Miranda's benefit as much as it would be mine.

As I wipe Roy's blood from my knuckles with the gag I'll stuff back into his mouth once he's given me what I need, I say, "Address. *Now.*"

"I—"

I hit him again, splitting the skin above his eye as effectively as the gash across his nose, before I pull a gun out of the back of my trousers and aim it to my left, right at the pinched pleat between my wife's brows.

"Address. *Now.* Or we're going to learn exactly how close you two became while scheming to play me for a fool."

Roy folds like a narc, and it reminds me of my true objectives.

None of them are for him.

13

MIRANDA

*A*s I twirl a pen between my fingers, I stray my eyes to my rapidly dwindling schedule. The pages were once full. Now they're covered with strikethroughs. My latest client's cancelation means I have only one event to cater for this month. Considering we're only weeks out from Christmas, that is extremely depressing to admit.

"I know it's late notice. But—"

"It's fine, Sawyer. I understand."

I don't, but what can I say? You shouldn't listen to anything my husband tells you because he'll use your lack of loyalty to the catering company you hired a year ago against you when he encourages your husband-to-be to file a last-minute prenuptial agreement.

A divorce attorney is no one's friend, so I have no clue why Roy's potential future victims are siding with him.

I would dig deep for answers if I weren't so angry.

Alas, I don't want to work with women who will cut off their nose to spite their face. I want to work with clients who respect and appreciate the effort I put in to make their event a huge success. I'm not a member of their staff or their employee. I am an extension of them and the love story they're trying to cram into a handful of selected dishes.

At the moment, only one couple on my once long list are giving me that vibe. It is for a wedding I'm meant to cater this weekend, the nuptials of Nikolai Popov and Justine Walsh.

Even arriving several hours late to our meeting this morning, and in a frazzled state, Justine assured me I have no true reason to cancel. She offered me the kitchen in the Popov mansion to prepare the feast for their guests and was happy to supply serving equipment.

If I accept her compromise, we will have to move the location of the wedding from the opulent gardens of the Popov mansion to the courtyard staff use for their lunch breaks and the occasional sneaky cigarette.

I don't want to do that. The gardening crew has been working on the grounds for months to get it ready for Justine and Nikolai's big day, and the hydrangeas were grown specifically to help conceal the large baby bump Justine doesn't want her childhood church minister to see.

A push back in dates would greatly assist both Justine and me, but Nikolai is adamant that they are to wed this weekend. Their babies—yes, you heard me right, they're having twins— aren't due for a couple more weeks, but Nikolai's intuition is warning him to wed now or watch his children enter the world as bastards.

I would have been appalled by his bigoted term if he had said it with any hint of harshness. I've never seen a groom-to-be more doting and obsessed with his wife-to-be as Nikolai is with Justine. He loves her wholeheartedly and wants to give her the world.

To him, that means Justine should share his last name when she births their children.

It's old-fashioned, but after reading the many gossip stories printed about Nikolai since the death of his father, it is understandable. He never had a stable, safe childhood. He was born in the ashes of hell and only began crawling out of them once he met Justine.

It makes me hopeful Nero comes through with the pledge he made hours ago. I'm rooting for the fairy tale Nikolai is envisioning for his unborn children and hope they never have to face the nightmares a lot of children unfairly endure these days.

I tune back in to my conversation when my latest cancellation continues harping on about how if she could change the outcome of her husband-to-be's decision, she would, but that it is out of her control.

"You know what the boys club is like, Myra." I don't get the chance to inform her of my real name. "Whether ten years since graduation or fifty, they always stand by each other's side. Your impending divorce will make my big day look messy."

I silently growl and bare teeth before I switch my voice from friendly to professional. "It is fine. Truly." A snippet of snarkiness slips through the cracks of my understanding. "I just hope you find someone willing to work with your budget in enough time. Fifty dollars a head is *well* below industry standards."

I only accepted Sawyer's stingy budget because eight out of

ten of her bridesmaids are single. Bridesmaids are prime catering game. We hunt them more than recently engaged brides-to-be because bridesmaids have faced the wrath of a Bridezilla and solemnly vow to *never* be like them.

Panic resonates more in Sawyer's tone now than it did when she called me to cancel an event that is only three weeks away. "What rate should I expect? Bill would like to keep things intimate."

By intimate, she means cheap.

"I'm not sure. I am only responsible for the quoting of events for my business."

My heart beats double time when Tempy's quick leap to her feet announces I have a visitor. She doesn't bark. She just races for the door with her tail wagging excessively.

"But I wish you well."

Before Sawyer can get in another word, I hit the end call button on my phone's screen, then twist in the direction Tempy raced.

As expected by the excited patter of her paws, my guest is welcome in my home.

Very much so.

As Nero drags his dark and brooding eyes down my body, his teeth get friendly with his bottom lip. I'm wearing a skirt I made indecent by cutting off the overhang Roy is adamant all women should have once married and paired it with my first, but unlikely last, sleeveless blouse.

My outfit is flirty and makes me feel very much like a woman who should be desired as much as she is respected.

"Hey, butterfly. You look pretty." Nero releases his lower lip with a moan as his lust-crammed eyes return to my face. "If I had known we were eating out, I would have dressed up."

He speaks as if he isn't wearing dressy slacks and a button-up shirt with the sleeves rolled to his elbows to show off his array of tattoos. His boots could use a polish since there are a handful of red splotches over them, but his hair is combed, his beard is trimmed, and he smells divine.

He looks sexy as fuck, and shockingly, our threads complement each other. His shirt is the same color as my blouse, and his slacks are a similar midnight black as my now-mini skirt.

The image of him in my doorway, waiting to be invited into my home instead of stomping over my privacy, makes my clit ache and has me grateful I decided to cook the meal I offered in exchange for his help instead of eating out.

Dessert is always quicker when you don't have to wait for the waiter to return to your table after you've finished the main course.

While striving to act like I'm not hopeful I will once again be Nero's dessert of choice, I open my screen door and officially invite him in before accepting the bottle of wine he's holding out. It is my favorite label, and its hefty price tag has me forgetting he distributes drugs and guns for a living and not art and antiques.

Although this will make me sound like a twit, I wasn't surprised when Shiloh shared some damning information about Nero and his many business dealings. He is well known by the locals in Vegas and extremely popular with adults her age.

I wasn't surprised because from the moment I'd laid eyes on Nero, he'd screamed danger. It's just never been directed at me long enough to cause the slightest tickle of fear to impede my speech, so I refuse to judge him on what society deems acceptable.

Nero's actions the afternoon we met, and the times that have followed, are what I will pay the most attention to.

Furthermore, I've done the man who's clean-shaven, would never get a tattoo, and would not tarnish his exemplary employment record by taking a single day off to swoon you.

It didn't work out.

He destroyed a decade of hard work in a weekend, and he doesn't appear anywhere near ready to end the brutal slaughter he's smacked my confidence with over the past fourteen years.

Roy wants me on my knees, and it is for a reason completely different from the one that fills my head when Nero's scent returns my focus to the present.

He stares at me until my heart returns to my chest instead of the floor Roy threw it on when I turned up at my warehouse to find it empty, and I've forgotten that the unseasonally barbaric heatwave in my kitchen has nothing to do with our location, and everything to do with him.

Then he kisses me.

Nero's mouth is warm, his lips are demanding, and his embrace as a whole is extremely claiming. It doubles the steaminess of my kitchen and has me wishing I had picked to forgo a bra when changing out of my work clothes.

Under-boob sweat is always worse when there's something to absorb it.

Our kiss is an inferno of touches, moans, and licks. It is as fiery as the flames that incinerated the legs of my once-marital bed, and I can't get enough.

I kiss Nero back with everything I have. The movements of my lips are just as claiming, my needs just as vocal.

It is a kiss so potent my thighs shudder and my clit throbs.

A kiss fantasies are made from.

It is the type of embrace that has me uncaring of a single person or thing not associated with the man breathing life back into my lungs one fire-sparking connection at a time.

My moans urge Nero on.

Before I know it, I go from the entryway of my home to being pinned to the wall oven in the kitchen.

My head is in such a tailspin, I'm barely grasping a sense of reality, let alone the pricy bottle of wine Nero arrived with.

"That was meant to be for when we get back," Nero says, talking over my kiss-swollen lips when the wine bottle tings against the wall oven. "But fuck if I can wait a second longer." He bites at my lips before he wedges his knee between my thighs, giving me something to grind against. "I'm hungry now."

The friction is delicious when I rub my damp panties against his muscular thigh. It steers me straight toward the finish line as productively as the tip of Nero's blade digs into the cork of the wine.

He pierces the cork before giving it a little wiggle, loosening it from the tight confines before his teeth wholly free it.

I smile like I'm a decade younger than I am when he spits the cork across the room like unnecessary messes are my jam before he tells me to open up.

When my lips part, I'm anticipating the rim of the bottle to cool the burn of his bearded kiss, so you can imagine my delight when I'm not served the wine from the bottle.

It is fed to me from Nero's mouth.

He swigs from the bottle, swirls the liquid around his mouth, doubling its flavors, before he tugs back my head by the roots of my hair and spits the wine into my mouth.

It tastes delicious, and I can't help but moan.

They gargle in my throat along with the wine when we share the equivalent of a glass with our mouths as the only utensils.

"Don't spill a drop, *printsessa*," Nero murmurs as he licks up a droplet of wine from my bottom lip. "I'd hate for your sexy little shirt to get stained."

With a confidence I'm still learning is okay to explore, I grip the hem of my shirt and pull it over my head.

Nero's hiss is as good this time around as it was when I wasn't wearing a bra.

His response makes sense when I lower my eyes to the bra he's edging as ruefully as his sexy face edges my horniness. The lace of the cups leaves nothing to the imagination, and the alluring baby-pink coloring adds a touch of sexiness to a usually bland palette.

"Mm," Nero moans, doubling the output of my heart. "Rosy and pink, just like your nipples."

He bites one of the said nipples through the scant material covering it before he rolls it between his teeth and tongue. Then, just as I'm about to beg, he pulls down the cup and doubles the stiffness with the coolness of the bottle's rim.

"Not a drop," I murmur when he tilts the bottle, bringing the liquid inside to the lip.

My knees knock when cool, fruity liquid rolls down my left breast half a second before Nero licks it up. His tongue is wide and enticing, and when it swivels around my nipple, it sends a current of electricity straight to my clit.

The coolness of the stainless-steel wall oven gives relief to my overheated skin when Nero follows the weave of a felonious droplet of wine. He tracks its movements down my stomach and its hazardous careen over my belly button before he catches it at the waistband of my skirt.

Goddamnit!

My fret is unwarranted.

"I'll buy you another one," Nero says two seconds before he shreds my skirt off my body, its flimsiness no match for the strength of his tug.

As my skirt sits tattered on the floor, he homes in on another defying droplet, its trek even more dangerous than its counterpart's.

It has slipped further down my body, almost to the waistband of my skimpy panties.

They're too scant to absorb the droplet and incapable of ignoring every heated breath that leaves Nero's mouth when he discards the wine bottle, his selection made.

My heart skips a beat when he hooks his index finger into the delicate edge of my panties before he slowly pulls the material away from my body.

He assesses me slowly and dedicatedly before his eyes float up my body. I'm panting hard and on the verge of hyperventilating when I realize how many lights are on in my kitchen, but he looks at me as if I am perfect—and I almost believe him.

"I so fucking wish you could see what I'm seeing right now."

He growls, and my hips jolt. I moan when my jerk forces his

nose to mash with my over-sensitive clit, and then I grunt when Nero loses all sense of control.

He spears his tongue between the folds of my pussy, doubling the shake of my thighs, before he drags it up to my clit.

A desperate squeak pops from my lips when he hits the nervy bud with back-to-back strikes.

With a handful of licks, he brings me to the edge so fast that I feel dizzy.

I won't fall. Nero's grip on my ass assures me of this, not to mention the leg he curls over his shoulder to open me more to him.

He distributes half my weight to his body and the other half to his tongue when he forces a flood of euphoria to race to my lower extremities from the expertise of his eating skills.

As his relentless pursuit to have me seeing stars ramps up, my hips instinctively roll. I grind my pussy against his mouth while his tongue demands the full attention of my clit.

"Give it to me, *printsessa*." Excitement zaps through me, his deep, rumbling voice enough to push me within an inch of the finish line. "Come on my face like a good little wifey."

Just the thought of him thinking I'm a good wife sees me losing the battle not to climax in a shamefully quick minute.

I buck like a bull while moaning his name in a mangled cry.

Tingles dance across my face while a tsunami wreaks havoc with my womb.

I can't stop coming, and Nero can't stop singing my praises.

He tells me how delicious I taste and that he's never sampled a more scrumptious meal. That he didn't think it was possible for me to get even more beautiful, but I defy the odds every time I come.

He builds me up so well that instead of crumbling into pieces when I come back from the lust cloud he forced my head into, my confidence grows along with the strength of my orgasm.

Roy never praised me. He never told me I was good at anything. He degraded me and made me feel worthless, so the thickness of the bulge in Nero's pants, and the desperateness in his tone to make me come undone, is addictive.

I feel wanted.

Needed.

I feel fucking invincible, and it is undeniable when I pluck Nero from the floor like he doesn't stand several inches taller than me and like the digits on my scale aren't higher than his.

As he kisses me like he knows his attention is reviving my lungs with air, I tug at Nero's belt and fumble with his zipper.

I pull away from his sinfully delicious mouth when his cock springs free from his pants. He's so thick, so hard, so mouthwateringly damp on the engorged tip that my train clatters off the tracks before my head hears the pleas of my body.

I fall to my knees and drag my tongue across the crown of his cock, sampling the evidence of his excitement, too impatient to wait.

Nero's grunt of approval surges my eagerness.

I grip him in my hand before feeding the first inch of his fat cock into my mouth. His heaviness both inside my mouth and in my hand makes me hot all over.

I'm both eager to please him and incredibly aroused that eating me has him hard enough to drill through to the Antarctic.

"Fuck, butterfly," Nero grunts when I take him to the back of my throat, his hips rocking.

I smile, loving the return of the nickname he only uses outside of the bedroom. It is as if he can see my wings expanding and my confidence soaring.

I suck him faster, greedily, dying to taste his cum once again.

I lose control, assured Nero will help me find my way back.

As Nero's hip thrusts double, his grip on my hair tightens. He tugs firm enough for the roots to sting, and I love every twinge of pain.

When I flutter my tongue down the vein responsible for the length and girth of his impressive manhood, his thigh muscles bunch as a cussword leaves his mouth. His free hand opens and closes as his head thrusts back.

He's close, so very close, and I am desperate to push him over the edge.

"Fuck."

His grunts come out thicker and stronger, as do the droplets of pre-cum leaking from the crown of his cock.

"Mir..."

His murmur of my name is cut short when I hollow my cheeks while swiveling my tongue around his cut crown. I suck gently, like his cock's head isn't throbbing with want, and then peer at him to marvel at his loss of control.

While maintaining eye contact, he rocks his hips faster, driving into my mouth with desperate, needy pumps.

My eyes bulge when he buries his cock a little too far, and tears spring, but I encourage the wildness beaming from him by flattening my tongue and relaxing the muscles in my throat, accepting him more profoundly.

He takes every inch of power I award him and thanks me for it by coating my taste buds with the deliciousness of his pre-cum. He fucks my mouth for several long minutes until the pointless gropes of my vaginal walls grow jealous by the attention my mouth is receiving.

I want him to fuck my pussy as hard as he is my mouth, and my prayers are answered two seconds after he pulls off his shirt like he's a member of the *Magic Mike* team and folds me over the kitchen island.

14

MIRANDA

*T*empy peers up from Nero's shirt she's claiming as her own when Nero enters me from behind with one swift thrust. She tilts her head and arches a brow, studying me as adeptly as Nero did when he was on his knees, peeling my panties down my thighs.

Only once she is confident my squeak is from pleasure, not pain, does she return her focus to Nero's shirt.

"Your dog is a perv," Nero says, his voice husky with lust as he unlatches my bra.

The straps fall to the counter as he weaves his fingers through my locks. The sting when he tugs my head back causes an avalanche of moans, and a handful of secrets, to spill from my mouth.

"Can you blame her? It takes everything I have not to flop out my tongue and drool anytime I see you. So someone who never leaves the house doesn't stand a chance."

I feel his laugh as much as I see it. It vibrates down his cock, making me ache, before it settles at my pulsating clit—the same clit that thuds maddeningly when Nero says, "Brace your foot on the drawer handle. I want to take you deep."

I do as asked before checking, "Here?"

He grunts in approval before he positions me to a more desirable pose. Then he re-enters me.

I've never felt small once in my life, but the way Nero towers over me, and how he moves me around without the slightest grunts of frustration, makes me feel small. I'd even go as far as saying tiny.

After giving me a second to acclimate to his size, he withdraws to the tip before he rams back in.

I moan, words above me.

I knew from the moment I laid eyes on him that he would be extraordinary in bed, but I had no idea it would be this good. This man is a machine built to give pleasure, and I'm the lucky bitch currently being served a slice of his brilliance.

I mewl when Nero slaps my ass cheek several long minutes later, reddening it, before he says, "Your ass, *printsessa*... fucking perfection." I'm blindsided by an unexpected orgasm when he murmurs his wicked thoughts out loud. "I can't wait to customize it to my cock. It will look so sexy wearing my marks, inside and out."

Once I've finished screaming through a toe-curling climax, my throat feels as raw as the chafe of my nipples from running back and forth over the marble countertop. It isn't a hurtful pain. More a realization of how much longer sex lasts when you're doing it for pleasure instead of a chore.

We've been fucking like a well-oiled machine for almost an hour. Even with foreplay, that was unheard of with Roy. He got off and then climbed off. Deed done.

The same can't be said for Nero. Our moves are synchronized and effortless, and our bodies are slicked with an even amount of sweat.

We fuck like we could be together for an eternity, and that the sparks will never diminish.

I could only pray to be so lucky.

As Nero drives me to the brink of ecstasy, his hips thrusting like he heard my negative thoughts, my moans ramp up from breathless to ear-piercing.

In minutes, I'm lost in the throes of lust, not a bad thought to be had.

I love how hard he takes me, and his impressive stamina. I truly believe that our mash-up is as pleasurable for him as it is for me. His grunts announce this, not to mention how thick his cock becomes when I show him my weight hasn't altered my flexibility.

I balance on my tippy-toes before lifting my right knee onto the kitchen counter, opening myself to him more.

When I peer back at him over my shoulder, the pure delight on his face is almost my undoing. I clamp down hard on his cock as shivers rake my spine.

"There's my butterfly," Nero murmurs when our eyes lock and hold while I tremor through signs of an earthshattering climax.

He winks like he knows my confidence thrives under his hooded watch, before he fucks me like a maniac. He pumps into me on repeat, stealing the air from my lungs while the walls of my vagina beg to milk his cock of his cum.

A familiar tightening stretches across my lower stomach when I see his struggle not to come written all over his face.

He likes what he sees as much as I do, and he is never one to hold back on the praise.

"Look at how well you're taking my cock, *printsessa*. You have me so hard my cum is going to rocket out of me and fill you up."

"Oh god," I pant when his next words make my mind spiral.

"I hope you're not ovulating, as you've got me so hard nothing will stop me from making you wholly mine. Not a pill...." *Thrust.* "Not a wife..." *Thrust.* "Not a man who had no fucking clue he had a plethora of perfection right under his nose for fourteen fucking years." *Thrust.*

I shake as waves crest in my stomach. Yes, waves. There are more than one.

Roy wouldn't even discuss the possibility of having a child until I was below one hundred and forty pounds. He said the risks were too high and that I needed to be below my goal weight to ensure I could get back to it after carrying his child for nine months.

He made it sound so unappealing that I thought motherhood wasn't for me.

Nero makes me feel different. He looks like he wants to impregnate me now, and in all honesty, if he asked, I doubt I'd object.

That's insane to admit, but it is the most honest I've ever been.

Fortunately, for the sake of my sanity that will inevitably

return once I'm no longer being screwed into oblivion, I've taken birth control religiously for fourteen years.

So, for now, this is purely about pleasure and the record number of orgasms Nero is willing to give me. It was five last night. I feel like today's efforts are going to stretch further than that.

My wild thoughts are proven accurate when Nero withdraws, flips me over, then buries his head back between my legs. "Still hungry. Need another helping."

15

NERO

*J*eat Miranda's delectable cunt until she screams my name twice and not an ounce of the numerous mistakes Swamp Dick made can be seen in her eyes. Then I step back.

I'm meant to be fucking her confidence to a record-breaking high, not making her bedridden.

Though the thought of her helpless and in bed for a week sounds mighty enticing right now. Miranda's pussy tastes like heaven. It's a meal I could eat day in and day out until the day I die, and I'd never complain.

Only a fool would grow tired of perfection.

As I drag a hand across my beard, making sure the wiry strands covering my jaw absorb her scent, I rake my eyes down Miranda's body.

We were so impatient I'm shocked the only article of clothing left on are my trousers, which are huddled around my ankles.

Other than that, we're stark naked, and the view is fucking enticing.

She's so damn beautiful. Her cheeks are flushed, her nipples are standing to attention, and although her pussy lips are red and chafed from my beard sanding the sensitive skin, they're drizzling with evidence of multiple arousals and make me hard as fuck.

The need to fuck claws at me. I want to take her hard and fast like when she was splayed over her kitchen counter, being pounded so ruefully her tits and ass clapped in euphoria. But for now, I can't. Miranda needs to see what she does to me. She needs to feel it.

She also needs to get that dweeb out of her head, and I know exactly how to encourage that.

I roll my thumb over her clit, keeping it as firm as my cock, while hooking my ankle around the leg of a chair beneath a nook at the side of the kitchen and dragging it in front of me.

Miranda's house has an old-school design, with part of the kitchen counter lowered to include a writing nook, but the fixtures and furniture are modern—excluding the piece I've selected.

Miranda watches me under hooded lids when I take a seat before notching up my chin, inviting her to join me.

She seems excited—for half a second.

"I'm not sure that chair was designed for two."

My voice is full of lust when I ask, "Afraid it'll break?"

When she nods, a smile stretches across my face.

She isn't distraught at the thought of her furniture being broken.

She's excited.

I learn why when she says, "That's Roy's favorite chair. He inherited it from his mother. She isn't dead. She just knows how much I hate that chair. I can't believe I missed it during my purge of his belongings."

I already knew Mrs. Martin is a steaming pile of shit—you can't raise a turd, shove a stick up its ass, and then call it a corn dog—but the disgust in Miranda's eyes exposes I still have a lot to learn about the Martins.

I'll start with his mother, once I've broken her god-ugly chair.

16

MIRANDA

*W*hen I throw the broken remains of my once-mother-in-law's chair into the trash can the garbage collection unit recently emptied, Nero's eyes stray to the firepit I've kept well-lit for the past week.

His eyes glow with as much enthusiasm now as they have with lust the past twenty-four hours when I say, "A proper burial seems too good for any belongings of *that* woman."

There's no deceit in my tone, no treachery, so Nero accepts my reply as if it is gospel before he holds out his hand in offering.

I can't recall the exact time he suggested we take a ride on his motorcycle, but since it was sometime between orgasm five and eleven, I stupidly agreed.

Cut me some slack. I've been riding the high of ecstasy for three days straight.

No one has smarts after one orgasm, let alone multiple.

While admiring the sexy curves of his pride and joy, I ask, "Are you sure you don't want to take my car? It's chilly out."

I'm such a liar, and Nero knows this. With an arched brow and a furled top lip, he curls his tattooed fingers around my wrist and tugs me forward until I either hook my leg over his bike or flop over the seat like I'm about to be spanked.

The idea of being spanked by Nero isn't unappealing, but since I'm just as curious to discover where he's taking me under the guise of a late-night ride, I slip onto the seat instead of lying across it, and then I curl my arms around his waist.

Nero's bike is as sexy as his face. It is dark, dangerous, and brooding. The rumbles of its engine when he kicks it over add to the throbs my pussy has been rarely without for the past week.

I nod like I'm not being eyeballed by a neighbor when Nero asks if I'm ready to go. Then I squeal. Nero's bike has a lot of power. It thrusts me back and reminds me that with the right amount of willpower, even the biggest obstacles can be pushed aside.

Take my marital status as an example.

Excluding the multiple times I've dreamed about arriving at the hotel ten minutes too late or using the gun I found minutes after discovering my cheating ex bound and gagged in a closet, Roy has barely entered my thoughts.

I can't wait to wash my hands of him. I just need to make sure Tempy isn't caught by friendly fire first, and then all cards are off the table.

I'll staple Roy's nuts to the wall.

Within minutes, the familiarity of my surroundings vanish, replaced with long stretches of road and heavily treed properties.

"You're not taking me out here to kill me, are you?"

I have to shout to ensure Nero can hear me. The wind is howling, and since neither of us are wearing helmets, there's nothing to protect our ears from the elements.

"I've heard stories about the woodlands that border the Popov mansion. Nothing good occurs here."

Nero laughs, aware the stories are the ones he's shared with me over the past two days. He stopped hiding who he was the instant I stopped letting society tell me what job titles they deem acceptable.

"If you are, can we play a game of chase first?"

I swallow my sass for a later date when we bypass a familiar street sign. It is for the main road of the Popov mansion, and it reminds me that I'm not meant to be living my best days when what should be the most important day of a couple's life is days away from being ruined.

It has been almost forty-eight hours since Nero offered to help me get the items I need to bring Justine's ideal wedding reception to fruition, but I haven't given him my list yet.

When I wrote down just the basics, it was obvious what I was asking was excessive.

Roy stripped my warehouse clean, leaving nothing but dust bunnies in his wake. I need everything from industrial ovens and the tents we use to shelter them while cooking to napkin rings and placement holders we place on every table setting.

As I battle my subconscious on whether I should accept Justine's offer to use the Popov kitchen or encourage her to use the backup catering firm I booked in case I have to renege on her offer, Nero steers his bike down a street several clicks up from the Popov mansion.

The road is dark and eerily quiet. There doesn't seem to be a single soul present... until the flashes of Nero's headlight switches on a hundred bulbs.

The outside of the building we slowly pull up to seems industrial, almost warehouse chic, but the cars and bikes outside and its internal features scream millionaire's lair.

I've heard there is a lot of money in the drug trade. I wouldn't have believed it until now. The wealth on display is crazy, and it makes me suddenly envious I took the straight and boring route instead of testing the stretch of people's leniencies.

I was born to be a rebel but settled for second best because I thought it was the right thing to do.

That's done with now.

After dismounting his bike more awkwardly than he straddled it, not wanting to accidentally kick me, Nero tosses his keys to a man with a gun strapped to his chest, before he lifts me off his bike. He once again makes it seem as if I am the weight of a feather.

When we head toward a group of men with obvious sneers and an array of dangerous weapons, only a micro part of me is scared.

This is far from the stuffy business get-togethers Roy never let me attend during our tumultuous marriage, but it has me more excited than terrified.

This is an equivalent of a workplace visit for Nero, and I'm delighted he's already reached a stage where he's happy to include me in *any* part of his life, let alone something obviously important to him.

The way he speaks of the Popov crew and his clear respect for its current heir makes it obvious these men and women are his family. He cares for them as much as he does his mother—and as I hope he one day will me.

As we enter the warehouse, we're awarded the eyes of everyone in the facility, including a handful of extremely skinny and practically naked women.

They're gorgeous, and for the first time in my life, I don't mentally chastise them. I return their smiles and revel in their confidence of loving the skin they're in.

With his hand curled around mine, his eyes nowhere near the numerous pairs of naked breasts, Nero asks, "Where's Eight?"

A man with a scruffy blond beard and numerous tattoos and piercings nudges his head to the right. "Doing inventory on stock we just acquired."

Nero jerks up his chin in thanks to a man with a British accent instead of the preferred Russian/American accent of the rest of the crew, before he heads in the direction he nudged.

He doesn't even get three steps away before the unease the man's thick beard can't hide slows his steps. "Do you think this is a good idea? Nikolai said only this morning that the investigation is still ongoing."

Nero *pffts* off his first sentence, but he struggles to ignore his second. "And I told Nikolai this afternoon that she has *nothing* to do with that."

So that's who his heated conversation was with this afternoon.

Since his call seemed work based, I stepped back and kept

myself busy. Only once it was done, and Nero was on the verge of exploding in anger, did I fumble into the role of caregiver as he has done for me numerous times whenever my confidence dipped below unbearable the past week.

Nero grips my hand so firmly that I almost yelp when the blond retaliates. "Do you think you're the best man to make that assessment? We're not meant to fuck the enemy, Nero. We're meant to destroy them."

Enemy?

Nero's smirk is menacing, and it pushes my inquiries as to my status in his life to the back of my head. "You, of all people, are judging my idea of what is right and wrong. Did you forget the little incident that occurred K's first night here?"

I don't know who K is, but the blond sure as hell does, and he isn't happy she's been brought into this fight. "Keep my wife's name out of your fucking mouth."

The bearded man looks set to rip Nero's head off with his bare hands, and I'm not the only one noticing. The crowd circles in close, hogging the premium seats.

Nero doesn't seem worried.

He looks like he has a ton of steam to burn off, and his target is locked and loaded.

I learn why when he spits out, "When you were lighting up her temple bright enough for everyone in Vegas to mistake it as the northern star, did she look like she had been here before, Trey? Did she have any fucking clue that you had the scope of your sniper locked on her fucking head like *I* did?"

Trey remains quiet, his expression a mix of peeved and pleased.

I tighten my fingers around Nero's hand before he can race across the concrete to force an answer from Trey, compelling him to use words instead. "Answer me! Did she look like she had been here before, or have any indication of the danger I was placing her in by trying to show you bunch of neanderthals that she isn't like the rest of them?"

"No," Trey eventually answers, his expression unreadable. "But Nikolai still won't like this."

"Then he can tell me that himself." Nero's voice is still dangerous. Still deadly. "Until then, step the fuck aside. This isn't your kingdom to guard."

While mumbling something about kingdoms being merely conquered provinces, Trey moves aside as requested.

My stomach gurgles when his soundless permission for us to enter Nikolai's realm is quickly chased by a man from the sidelines hooking his leg over an all-terrain vehicle and taking off in the direction of the Popov residence.

He wears tattler as obviously as I wear worry.

"I don't need to be here," I say to Nero, halving the lengths of his strides.

His narrowed eyes widen the longer they float over my worried expression. "They won't hurt you, butterfly. They were ordered not to months ago. They won't disobey a direct order. Not from Nikolai or myself."

"I'm not worried about me." Nothing but honesty rings in my tone.

I trust Nero because why would he build me up so high only to stand back and watch me be knocked down? It is the intentions of others I am worried about.

In between the wild, crazy sex, and a sickening number of calories to keep our energy up, we talked—a lot.

Years of stories were spilled in hours. Nothing was off-limits, and the purge brought us so close you'd swear we've been dating for months.

If we're even dating.

Nero scoffs as if he heard my thoughts. It doesn't match his smirk when he asks, "Then who are you worried about?"

"You," I answer without pause for contemplation, speaking from my heart as I have numerous times over the past four days. "And how many people Tasha hooked with her nails while she was here."

I've been ruminating over Tasha's game plan since Nero explained the swiftness of their marriage and how it came about. I don't trust her as far as I can throw her.

I reconsider my analogy after remembering how tiny she is.

I don't trust her. Period.

Nero's smile turns genuine, and it makes my knees quake for a completely different reason than my worry that we're walking into a trap.

"If that's the case, butterfly, you've got *nothing* to worry about." He continues walking, taking me with him. "She's never been here, and she will *never* be invited to come here."

I don't bother hiding my delight that I've progressed further than his quickie Vegas marriage. He can't see my smile since he is in front of me—though you wouldn't know that from how clammy his hand gets when I set it free.

My heart is already in a state of disrepair, but it surges to coronary failure territory when we pass through thick plastic curtains at the side of a warehouse. All the catering products I wrote down, and a handful of missed ones, stretch from one wall to the next.

Everything I need to bring Justine's wedding reception to its glory is in this room. He even sourced the engraved caviar spoons most guests don't know how to use.

"How?" My mouth moves, but that is all that comes out.

I'm too shocked to speak.

I didn't give him my list, so how did he get everything I need?

I'm torn between hollering in excitement and growling in anger when Nero answers, "The buyer Roy sought was a friend of a friend. He had no clue he was purchasing stolen goods. He thought it was a regretful sale of a once-loved business because of the dissolution of a marriage."

I talk through the lump in my throat when the entirety of his reply works through the lust haze stealing my smarts. "This is *my* stuff?"

Nero nods, and the nonchalance of his response makes me laugh. It is highly inappropriate, but it is either laugh or tackle him to the floor and let him impregnate me like the desire shouldn't only ruminate from the exhaustion of multiple orgasms.

Regretfully, I go for what I believe society will find acceptable for a woman still technically married.

"Will Roy get in trouble for this?" I pick up a napkin holder I purchased specifically for Nikolai and Justine's wedding before twisting to face Nero. "I don't care about what happens to Roy. I'm just curious as to the process of selling stolen goods to someone in the mafia."

"Bratva," Nero corrects. "This is the bratva."

He twists his kissable lips, disappointing me that I went for the route society deems acceptable even after he's proven time and time again the past week that it isn't close to what I crave.

"And I guess it depends."

"On?" I ask, his reply seemingly unfinished, and fighting like hell not to backflip on my earlier decision.

Nothing but honesty rings in his tone when he steps so close to me that I can smell my perfume on his skin. "On how you want to punish him." He frees my lower lip from my menacing teeth before he says, "He stole *your* belongings, butterfly. So you're the only one who can choose his punishment."

I place down the engraved napkin ring before stepping closer to him. I'm grateful for the natural rub of my thighs. I need something to take the edge off before I make a fool of myself.

"Is that how it usually works in the bratva?"

With how fast the bulge in Nero's crotch grows, you'd swear I moaned my last word while climaxing. That's how rapidly his cock thickens from my underhanded respect of his world.

"Is the person who was hurt always the judge of their perpetrator's punishments?"

My answer doesn't come from Nero. It is from a voice outside the room. "Not always... but a king who respects his queen is always open to compromise."

My heart patters in my ears when Nikolai enters the room. He has the swagger of a man who knows how attractive he is but also the aura of a mass murderer. Unlike the times we've met previously, when his wife-to-be was present, he screams danger and is extremely on edge.

After taking in my flushed cheeks and Nero's balled hands, Nikolai shifts to his left. "Is everything here?"

Again, the chance to answer is given by an outside source. "From what I can see, yeah."

A guy who'd have to be at least seven feet tall joins our trio, plumping it out to a quartet. I've seen him previously, though we've never officially met. He was behind the steering wheel of the vehicle Nero was seated in when I exited the hotel.

"Though I wouldn't say no to a second look from someone in the know."

When everyone's eyes shift to me, I melt like a popsicle on a hot summer's day.

It isn't in a good way.

Nero's gaze is still hooded, but some of the lust brimming in his eyes only moments ago has switched to anger, meaning they now house as much unease as Nikolai and the unnamed man hold.

They're hard for me to read. I can't tell if they're looking at me as their friend or the enemy Trey warned Nero about earlier.

"Um..." I swallow to replenish my throat with spit before saying, "We did a stock take recently to prepare for tax season. I have a copy of the report on my laptop..."

My words trail off when the unnamed man hands me the printout he's clasping. It is an itemized list of the items in my warehouse, an exact replica of the one I typed up.

"Where did you get this?" I ask, the printout too familiar to discount.

It is from *my* laptop. I have no doubt about that.

"Answer Eight's question first," Nero says, his tone a mix of danger and seduction. "Then we will move on to smoothing that groove between your brows, butterfly."

My libido surges from his underhanded comment that we're about to get frisky, but for once, my brain overrules it.

"Have you been spying on me?"

"Butterfly—"

"Answer me, goddamnit!" I shout, too angry about having my feelings stomped on over and over again to realize I am taking my frustration out on the wrong people.

Nikolai looks like he wants to slit my throat. Eight appears amused. But Nero... he looks like he wants to devour me where I stand, one perfectly placed lick, bite, and poke at a time.

My backbone turns him on, so it is only fair I give him some of the sass he's worked hard to unearth in an astonishingly quick time.

"Everything on the list appears to be here except..."

I wait until the tension reaches its boiling point, and then I curve a brow, wordlessly announcing I'm not speaking another word until I'm given something in return for my efforts.

Eight breaks the intense stare down first. "Aight. I'll bite." He rubs his hands together while shuffling from foot to foot. "We've misplaced something. We're of the belief you have it." After gesturing his hand between Nikolai and himself, he nudges his head to Nero. "Nero believes differently."

I appreciate both his honesty and belief that Nero has faith in me, but it doesn't alter the facts.

I'm being eyeballed as if I am the criminal half of our duo.

"How long ago did your... *stuff* go missing?" I want to ask how long I've been under surveillance, but it is less heart-breaking this way.

It is a fight not to fold in two when Nikolai answers, "Four days ago."

"Which was a good twelve months *after* Nero purchased the house across the street from you so he could make out he isn't mowing another man's turf by stroking his cock to his missus from afar." Eight's lips snatch shut when Nero growls. "What? I thought she knew." He swallows harshly before shifting his eyes to me. "How do you think he changed so fast tonight? Tempy wasn't giving up his shirt for anything, even with it reeking of sweat, and the winds are too cold to go shirtless on a motorcycle, so he popped home for two seconds to get dressed, most likely for the first time in days, while you rustled up a pair of fitted jeans from the back of your closet."

I can't fight the urge to bend for a second longer.

He's been watching us.

Does that mean he saw us...

I can't say it.

I refuse.

I'm also devastated by what his confession could mean. I thought Nero was attracted to me because he saw past the stigma of being with a plus-size woman. I had no clue he was only sniffing around to find the goods his boss believes I stole.

I've never felt more stupid.

"Could you make it sound any more perverted, fuckface?" Nero snaps out, his fury undeniable. "He was watching you, butterfly. But only because I asked him to keep an eye on you. I had to know you were safe when I wasn't there. But he only had access to the cameras monitoring the outside of your home. He didn't have access to anything behind closed doors. I'd kill him before I'd ever let him see you like that."

I want to believe him, but four plus four doesn't equal ten.

"Then how does he know Tempy claimed your shirt?"

Eight answers before Nero can. "She dragged it onto the patio this afternoon so she could nestle with it next to the firepit and in the low-hanging sun."

Oh. I'm still angry, but Tempy loves heat, and the temperature in our home cooled drastically when Nero took his call, so his excuse is believable.

There's just one thing that doesn't make sense.

"What's your excuse for knowing I wrestled my jeans out of the back of my closet?"

Now, I'm not the only one angry. Nero looks furious, and his I'm-going-to-kill-you stare has Eight speaking at the speed of sound. "Her ex is a douche. He's been giving her shit all week. When I shut him up with my fists, the front of his pants got a little stained. I figured I'd replace them with a pair from across the street, forgetting she had burned all his belongings, including his ugly-ass suits." He shifts on his feet to face me. "I saved myself a trip to the store by compromising with a pair of jeans I found in the back of your closet." His smile is unexpected considering the heat of our exchange. "For someone who thinks meat on bones is for dogs, your husband's new threads are an extremely snug fit."

"Soon to be *ex*-husband," Nero chimes in, not wanting anyone to confuse his dislike of cheaters.

As I drift my eyes between three sets, I suck in some big

breaths. There's too much to take in. I'm the most confused I've ever been, but somehow, also curious.

"Don't," I snap out, pulling away when Nero attempts to bring me out of my stupor state with touch.

I'll never work through my confusion with that man's hands on me, and I'm suddenly sickened by the idea instead of hopeful.

Once I've sucked in a lung-filling breath, attempting to weaken some of the fog in my head, I twist to face Nikolai, the man I'm reasonably sure is responsible for Nero's resurrection in my life.

"I don't have your... *stuff*. Everything that was in my warehouse is here..." I pause again. This time, more from the sudden realization not everything Shiloh and I counted during stock take is present on the inventory list. "Except the commercial bags of flour I purchased for your wedding. Justine wanted the guests served freshly made Prizohkis. They require a *lot* of flour."

"Flour?" Nikolai asks, his brows pulled together. "That's all that is missing from your inventory. Just flour?"

I nod, words above me.

As he works his jaw side to side, Nikolai twists to face Nero. I'm torn between throwing myself in front of Nero's body and saving myself when Nikolai's eyes narrow into thin slits.

Luckily for me, death stares can't kill, so I don't have to deliberate on a choice that shouldn't require deliberation.

"Were the bags of flour in her warehouse when they first searched for the coke checked?"

Nero's dark eyes snap to Eight, who suddenly looks mighty uncomfortable. "I thought it was flour, so I didn't bother." Nikolai growls, so Eight talks faster. "It's just fucking flour—"

"Yes, that's right. It's *just* fucking flour." Nikolai mocks his non-Russian accent. "Which is how we get *it* past customs with no fucking issues!" After a quick grind, Nikolai orders Eight to take some men to my warehouse to check the authenticity of the product in the bags of flour, and then he shifts his focus to Nero. "Take your girl home."

Too hurt to not respond, I murmur, "I'm not his girl."

Nikolai acts as if I never spoke. "This appears more a mix-up with shipping than blatant disrespect of my authority."

He goes to leave, but something stops him.

I realize it is me when Nero pulls me behind him before I can protest.

While smirking like he isn't surprised by Nero's protectiveness, Nikolai says, "Don't make me remind her of the consequences when someone upsets my *ahren*." It is a struggle to hear what he says next. That's how loud the grinding of Nero's teeth is when Nikolai's threat picks up steam. "Sort your shit out, and then have you and your girl on deck Friday afternoon to bring Justine's dreams to fruition Saturday night."

"That's only days away," I push out, too shocked not to speak. "He'll need a lot longer than that to fix the mistakes he's made."

Nikolai's smile announces why Justine fell in love with him so fast. It is as corrupt as it is knee-wobbling, and it exposes he is a man with many sides.

"I've worked with less."

Not looking back, he leaves me alone with Nero and too much anger not to displace.

17

NERO

 $\mathcal{M}$ y jaw cracks when Miranda puts enough power behind her swing to knock any man on his ass. Birds fly around my head as a headache instantly forms. But I remain standing—just.

I work my jaw side to side to make sure it isn't broken before righting my head.

Upon spotting the welt on my face, Miranda stares at me with her mouth open and her eyes wide. She didn't think she had it in her to retaliate with violence.

I've always known it.

From the moment I laid eyes on her, I knew she had it in her to tell her emotionally and verbally abusive husband to step the fuck back with more than words. Her gall was just hidden beneath years of manipulation and society's wrong beliefs of perfection.

That's done with now.

"You good, butterfly? Or do you want to weapon up to save your pretty hand from getting nicked up?"

She swings again. I dodge this one before I use her imbalance to pull her into my body and lock down her missile-serving arms.

"Let me go!" she screams, her voice echoing even with the warehouse brimming with the goods her husband stole from her.

I don't heel to her shouted command.

I hold on tight, loving her fight.

There's nothing sexier than a woman with enough gall to put a grown-ass man in his place.

The thickness of my cock is heard in my words. "I will let you go... when you make me."

"Ugh!"

Miranda screams, kicks, and scratches. Then she bites. That defense move turns me on the most. It is as possessive as it is aggressive, and proves she knows deep down that our hookups over the past few days haven't been about searching for the fifteen-million-dollar cocaine shipment that went awry when I was taking out the trash striving to make her an overnight online sensation, and everything to do with an obsession a year in the making.

Yes, I stalked her.

Yes, I stroked my cock while watching her move from the gym in her garage to her loft-like bedroom, removing her clothes on the way.

Yes, I wanted her from the moment I saw her.

But I didn't force her to become a part of my life.

I stood back and made sure she was safe. Then the name of her catering business fell into my lap.

That was three days *after* we slept together.

Coincidence? Un-fucking-likely. But I wasn't going to sidestep the perfect opportunity to show this beautiful, cock-thickening woman that she deserves far better than a weasel like Roy Martin.

I just had to perfect the work-life balance my personal life has been without for over two decades.

The hours I wasn't with Miranda, I've been striving to find the missing coke and who threw her name into the hat when I got too close to the truth. It can't be Roy or Tasha. They've been under my captivity the entire time, so it has to be someone else—someone not even Miranda would consider looking at.

The gleam Eight's eyes got when he was told to revisit Miranda's warehouse has wild curls and chubby cheeks popping into my head—and a heap of unfounded theories.

"What was the name of your assistant, again? The curvy one with the curly hair."

Miranda kicks out so hard that I'm almost emasculated.

She almost takes out my dick.

"Don't you dare bring Shiloh into this. She hasn't done anything wrong."

I adjust her to protect my nuts before saying, "If she means something to you, she means something to me, butterfly, so you have my word that I won't do shit to her."

Eight, on the other hand...

I'm pulled from uncalled-for thoughts when Miranda shouts, "How can a shipping kerfuffle be blamed on anyone but the shipping company? Nikolai said it was a mistake!"

"Nikolai is a man in love. He's about to marry his angel and watch her birth his kin. He isn't thinking with his head right now. That's why I need to have his back."

As much as this kills me to admit, I now have a better understanding of Trey's concerns.

I'm just as snowed under as Nikolai, if not more.

When you're finally lucky enough to test something you've craved for months, you fall for its wizardry fucking fast.

I'm under Miranda's spell, and not at all ashamed to admit that.

Miranda's words rip from her mouth. "Oh, right. Sorry. I forget fucking someone below your league is how men like you take one for the team!"

Nothing but fury resonates in my tone. "What the fuck did you just say?"

I don't care about her insinuation men in my industry use their dicks to get what they want. That's a well-used tactic in any ruses that involve women. I'm pissed as fuck to her alluding that she's below me.

I stayed away after her cocoon cracked because I know she's too good for me. I didn't want her wings sullied so soon after they were freed. I struggle to keep my hands to myself when she's in the vicinity. She's the flame and I'm the moth. Our wings aren't close to the same caliber, so I tried to do the right thing.

Tried—the ultimate summit of my viewpoint.

I can't do it anymore.

The instant Miranda knew my wings were more devilish than angelic, and she didn't press on the brakes, this train moved forward at a dangerous speed.

I refuse to give her up for anything or anyone—even men I've known over half my life.

"You heard me," Miranda spits out, still fighting, still drawing me in with her grit. "That's why you showed up at my doorstep, isn't it? You arrived looking for the missing cocaine and thought, *What the hell, what's one more pity fuck?*"

I let her go, happy to face the wrath of her fury if it gives me her eyes. They are the only things capable of displaying her true feelings. They show the woman behind the shield her fuckface of a husband forced on her years ago.

Miranda spins on a dime and whacks into my chest, too enraged with anger to pay attention to the caution in my tone.

Nothing will stop her onslaught—except a warning she knows I will uphold to the letter.

"Every whack, bite, scratch, and nick you do to me, I'll do back to you. That's how we operate. That's our thing."

"*Our?*" She scoffs as if disgusted. It is a pity her scent announces differently.

She is as turned on right now as I am, and one step from waving the white flag.

"Yes. *Our.*"

Before she can respond with the fierceness I've craved from her since the day I laid eyes on her, I snake my hand up her back, fist her locks, then seal my mouth over hers.

There's nothing tender about my kiss. Nothing friendly. It is possessive and claiming, a kiss that speaks my intentions better than words ever could.

And Miranda is defenseless to its onslaught.

"Does this feel like the reaction of a man pity fucking?"

I grip her ass and rock my hips forward, dragging my erection against her heat, drawing out her sultry moans.

"I stayed away at the start because I *know* you deserve better than both the douche you *once* called your husband and me. But don't take that as disinterest on my behalf. I had eyes on you more than on my job. That's how they were able to play me for a fool. *Again.*"

Conflicting timelines removed the nooses from Roy's and Tasha's necks for the missing cocaine, but something isn't adding up. There are too many missing pieces to this puzzle, but not enough hours in the day to find them.

The number of bullets I'm dodging should have my cock hanging limp, but this, my butterfly's final metamorphosis, is more important than insolent idiots too dumb to remain hidden forever.

They'll start acting flashy and will talk shit like all unaccredited drug mules do, and then I'll take them down. It will only be *after* they've announced who suggested Miranda's business name should be dropped into the dirt with them, though.

After reacquainting our lips, I kiss Miranda with everything I have.

Several long minutes pass before I pull back to marvel at the life firing through her pretty eyes.

"Every time I have you, I want you more."

My tongue lashes her kiss-swollen lips, still craving more even when she is right in front of me.

"The first time I saw you... *fuck.* Your beauty brought me to my knees. Then, as I watched you more and more, I realized your attractiveness goes much deeper than skin deep. Everything about you is perfect. Your smile, your kindness, your ability to make it seem as if you're happy even when you're dying on the inside."

I kiss the edge of her mouth for each statement, tinging their honesty with a smear of deceit, but too desperate to touch her to hold back for a moment longer.

"But you weren't mine to do with as I pleased. Both on paper and in your eyes, you belonged to another man." She tries to interrupt me, so I speak faster. "So I kept my distance and bided my time, knowing one day you'd eventually break out of your cocoon and be free of him." Again, I inch back, smirking when she groans. "I couldn't force you to do that, though. Your metamorphosis had to be your own doing. It made you that much stronger." The lust in her eyes announces she is aware of my next sentence before I articulate it. "Strong enough to know you could stop this if you truly want to."

I use my grip on her hair to force her to her knees, and then I use my opposite hand to raise her chin and lock our eyes.

When I drag my thumb over her lips, softening them to be stretched, she whimpers. It drills through the last of my resistance and has me speaking as honestly as I have the past forty-eight hours.

"The only person about to be pity fucked is me. But fuck if I can stop this, butterfly. I crave you enough to watch you from afar for a year and keep my hands to myself. There ain't no way I'll achieve the same now knowing I can have you. I crave you more than my lungs crave air. You're my drug of choice."

With her wings fully expanded, Miranda gets on board with my plans rather quickly. One second, she's wetting her lips. The next, she's tugging on the fastener of my jeans and pulling my cock out of my pants.

I groan when her plump lips circle my crown, and then my teeth crunch when she takes me to the back of her throat.

For a woman who was never given the chance to showcase her brilliance of giving head, her skills are undeniable.

Miranda knows how to please a man orally.

I'd be jealous as fuck if I had witnessed a single scenario instigated by lust with her husband.

In the twelve months I stalked her, I didn't even see them kiss once.

"Christ..." I grunt when she swivels her tongue around the base of my cock and fights past her gag reflex to accept me as deeply seated as possible. "You're taking me so deep."

I gather her hair in a ponytail, then use the firmness of my hold to control the movements of her head. I can't have her choking on my cock, even with her gags sounding like calls from heaven.

When I say that to Miranda, her moan vibrates down my shaft, making me thicker.

Pre-cum leaks from the top of my cut penis as she sucks the marrow from my bones. She licks it up, as desperate for my taste as I am hers. I want her to ride my face, and for her juices to drench my beard, but I need her to feel how hard she makes me.

She needs to know none of this is about anyone else but us.

Miranda's eager sucks have me racing for the finish line. She pays a heap of attention to my engorged crown while pumping the portions of my shaft missing out on the warmth of her mouth.

Then, just as my balls pull in close to my body, she kneads the pressure making our exchange painful.

I've never wanted to come so badly in my life.

My grunts and moans encourage Miranda to go faster. She loses control on my cock, and it takes everything I have not to surrender to the madness. I want to come down her throat, to watch her eyes dilate as I spill my load onto her tongue, but I also want to be balls deep inside her before filling her with my sperm.

Taking her bare gets better every time we do it. The dangers associated with unprotected sex, and the knowledge she is the only woman I've ever broken the rules for, has me putting steps into play to experience it again before they've fully ruminated.

In ten heart-thrashing seconds, I flip Miranda over until she is on her hands and knees and her fantastic ass is thrust high in the air, unbutton her jeans, peel the waistbands of her jeans and panties to her knees, then enter her from behind with one ardent thrust.

She calls out, her moan unlike anything I've ever heard. It has my cock throbbing through a release like I won't be ridiculed to hell for coming after one pump, but I don't stop. I continue pounding into her until her climax hits as fast as mine smashed into me.

As I pound into her relentlessly, she shouts my name.

Shivers wrack her body, and the walls of her pussy tighten around my shaft.

"*Yesss...* Take me. Accept every inch. Swallow my dick like you're still hungry for my cum."

My cock thickens to the point it is painful when the angle of our romp allows me to see the mix of our excitement on the shaft of my unsheathed cock.

"Oh god..." Miranda moans, her words breathless and full of lust as she slowly comes down from climax. "How are you still so hard? You're taking me so deep. It feels so good."

My chest puffs high, proud of the shock in her tone.

"It's you, butterfly. Everything about you makes me hard."

I thrust fast, making her tits clap.

"And then there's contemplating if his plan will work, but for me instead of him."

Miranda peers back at me with red cheeks and wide eyes.

Her confusion should lessen the strength of my pumps.

It doesn't.

It doubles them.

I'm not a jealous fuck... until it comes to her.

Then I'm a fucking tyrant.

"There was only one time I intervened in your marriage before you invited the carnage." I fuck her wildly, like she is to blame for her husband's fucked-up ideas of marital bliss. "I didn't give a fuck that you had his last name. There was no way I was going to let a prick like *him* knock you up."

Miranda's mouth pops open to release a moan in response to my brutal pounds, but eventually, a handful of words slip out between her heavy breaths. "Roy... doesn't... want... children."

I grind my teeth together before forcing words between them. "Then why did he replace your birth control with placebos?"

She wiggles, demanding I stop.

There's no fucking chance in hell of that happening. I held back my desires for months for that prick. I ain't doing it again.

As I continue thrusting, shifting the concern on Miranda's face to need, she slowly says, "I don't know."

Another handful of pumps.

Another husky sentence.

"But I promise it wasn't for what you're thinking." She shivers through signs of an imminent orgasm before continuing. "For one, we'd need to have sex for *that* to happen"—I stop punishing her for the foolhardiness of another when she adds—"and we've not done that in an *extremely* long time."

I slow the thrusts of my hips until they're no longer manic, and then I slide my hand around her body to toy with her clit.

The swivels of my index finger and middle finger, and the flexes of my cock as I stretch her wide, switch the focus back to where it should have never deviated from.

It returns it to us.

A low, shallow groan rolls up my chest when Miranda's moans remind me of the faint noises she releases when she is consuming something naughty. Before I entered her life with guns blazing—literally—it was only ever in the darkness of night and long after her husband went to bed.

"Mm."

I doubt she knows she's doing it. She is too self-conscious after years of abuse to openly express her desires, but they're the noises I crave more than her screams.

They expose the true depth of her pleasure, and how they only ever sound now when I am near.

As our wild fuck soothes to lovemaking, Miranda's little mewls pick up. They clutch at my throat as vigorously as her pussy clutches my cock.

Who knew something so simple could bring a man to his knees?

"I need you to come again, *printsessa*. I need you nice and wet to make my sperms' swim effortless."

"Nero..." Her husky delivery of my name makes her seem cautionary. Her body is on the opposite end of the spectrum. It stills for half a second before it shakes in the brilliance of a fire-sparking climax.

Miranda moans my name again, louder this time, as the tight clamps of her pussy set me off. I come with a roar, my cock throbbing as sperm rockets out of me.

Then I realize we're not alone two seconds before Miranda.

18

NERO

"*I* swear on my middle finger's life, I didn't see shit."
Eight nervously shifts from foot to foot, weakening the honesty of his statement.

He's called Eight because he's a fucking giant, often seeming closer to eight feet than seven, he was born in the eighth month of the year, his given name is August, and he has only eight fingers.

Eight swears one of his finger removals was an accident.

He won't tell anyone about how he lost digit number two.

He has no reason to lie, but I appreciate his endeavor to pull me over the fence. "You were way too up in her business to get the slightest peek. Can't say I blame you. Your girl is *fine*."

Miranda, who I know has been listening in from the start since her perfume grew more noticeable when Eight knocked on the door of my room in the Clark's compound to issue his tenth apology, giggles during his last statement.

I veer my fist toward his eyes.

"Jesus fucking Christ. I was giving her a compliment. Not an invitation to my bed."

"I don't give a fuck. Keep your beady eyes off my woman. Clothed or naked."

While *pffting* like I have no reason for my anger, he hands me a wadded piece of paper. When our eyes lock, he silently pleads for me to open it in private.

When I nod, suddenly remorseful that my jealousy has me seeing friends as enemies, Eight pivots on his heel and stalks down the corridor.

He's partway down when I try to make up for his bloody nose. "She's single."

He cranks his neck back to face me, his smile announcing he appreciates my extension of an olive branch but that he has no intention of letting me off easily. "Who?"

I play stupid as well as I do jealous. "A giant doesn't want a boneless carcass to feast on. He needs meat. Lots of *juicy* meat."

It's fucked to admit this while standing across from my brother in arms, but I'll never be a man who tiptoes around the truth. I much prefer stomping on it.

I'm hard as stone and uncaring who knows it since my room door has a lock, and the woman from my dreams is making herself at home in my domain.

With a grin of a serial killer, Eight says, "I'll buy you an hour. Any longer than that, you're on your own."

His reply has me wishing he was dead. Eight only knocks at your door when you're being summoned. That summoning only occurs around here by one man. Nikolai.

This kills me to admit, but I never thought the day would come where I'd put a woman above my loyalty to Nikolai.

Today is that day.

When Nikolai underhandedly threatened Miranda, I almost lost my shit. It was only when I recalled why his guards are up did my anger sit the fuck down.

He wasn't pissed about the massive hit his empire just took, or that someone is playing him for a fool. He's worried about Justine and how she will handle the best caterer in the state playing hooky on her big day.

He wants to protect his *ahren* from a bucketload of disappointment as readily as I'm striving to do the same for my butterfly.

After a quick work of my jaw, I open the note.

As expected, it is from Nikolai.

Need to see you at P's.
Bring your girl.

When I flick my eyes up, my thoughts a mix between fuck no and double fuck no, Miranda strays her eyes to mine. She's holding an invoice in her hand, and a deep groove is scoured between her dark brows.

"Did you witness Roy replace my birth control pills, or did he tell you he did that?"

I grind my back molars together to lessen the severity of my scorn while pacing closer to her. "I witnessed him do it."

"When?" She doesn't sound angry. She is more curious than anything.

I think back to the numerous times I saw her almost build the courage to leave him before I rewind back to the only time he gave me any indication he wanted to keep her for himself.

"It was around a month ago. You'd gone out for a run in that hideous sweater he was adamant you had to wear over your workout clothes. He extended the route on your running app so you'd be gone long enough for him to change your birth control pills."

She looks torn between kissing me and strangling me.

Or perhaps she wants to kiss me and strangle her husband.

I much prefer the latter.

"I snuck inside in the middle of the night to change them back, and then I got blind fucking drunk."

When the light finally switches on, Miranda has no trouble deciphering the facts. "Because you hated the thought that he still wanted me, which meant you couldn't have me." She smirks like she's shocked I haven't slotted the pieces together as quickly as she has. "When Roy told me the house across the street had been sold to an investor wanting to flip it when the market improved, I was devastated. I met your mother when she came to approve the remodel of the house her only son had purchased for her. She was so excited about the rebuild, so to hear it wasn't going through, I grew worried something terrible had happened to her." Her smile almost buckles my knees. "My devastation mimicked hers when I tracked her down in a brand-new condo a few streets over and she learned I was married. I hadn't been wearing my wedding ring the day we met."

As her eyes spark with love, she continues her story. "Apparently, I was exactly her son's type, but there was no hope for us.

She said he would never mow another man's turf, no matter how untidy his yard, because she had raised him better than that." Her expression is an odd mix of lusty and understanding. "What changed your mind?"

"It wasn't a what. It was a who." I step closer, hating the minute few feet between us. "His betrayal should have destroyed you. It should have broken your spirit." Pride puffs out my chest. "It didn't. Your cocoon was already cracked when you arrived at the hotel." I cup her cheeks and drag my thumb over her lips. "He had finally lost you, so there was no reason I couldn't help you find yourself again."

"This isn't a game of finders keepers, Nero."

I scoff, confident as fuck that I'll have her believing differently in a matter of minutes if forced to express myself with more than words.

"But even if it is, you were also married."

"On paper. Not in my eyes or in the eyes of my mother. My divorce is close to being completed."

"Close... but *not* finalized." Her smarts exceed her beauty for half a second. "Why was the annulment denied?"

I'm lost as to where she is going with this and what the invoice she is clutching has to do with it, but I'm willing to play along if it keeps her wings fanned as wide as they are now.

"Even strung out and drunk, I was still smart enough to request a prenup. The infidelity clause of said prenup is why the annulment was denied. Tasha told the judge she would have proof that I'd cheated at our next mediation hearing, which is scheduled for some time next month."

"*Would* have? Not had?"

I nod, still confused.

My bewilderment doubles when Miranda smiles at me like it is Christmas morning and I found her under my tree, wrapped in nothing but a bow, before she asks, "Where are you keeping them?"

"Them?" I ask, acting daft.

I've shared a lot of dark and demented shit with her the past few days, but I've kept Roy's captivity on the down-low. I don't want her learning that I am a complete fucking psycho before she's fully under my spell.

I can't pull the wool over her eyes, and in all honesty, I don't want to.

"*Our* cheating spouses, Nero. Where are they?"

Against my better judgment, I nudge my head to the door. "Let me show you." With her confidence too high to topple, I add, "We just need to make a quick detour first."

19

MIRANDA

*S*oot, dust, and a smell I can't quite recognize filter into my nose when I follow Nero into the basement of the house across the road from my home. I could blame it on the untouched onion rings sitting beside empty takeout containers on a black TV stand dinner tray, but the stain in the front of Roy's pants won't allow it.

He's ruining what I'd hoped would become my favorite pair of skinny jeans with more than a voluptuous frame, and the situation worsens when anger isn't the first thing to flash through his eyes when they land on me.

It isn't even wordless begs for help.

It is a lusty glint a man as dominant and claiming as Nero will never sweep under the carpet.

A crack sounds.

It is closely followed by a groan.

Oddly, I don't cringe when the removal of Roy's gag, so he

doesn't choke on the blood Nero's fist forced from his nose, is chased by a tooth being spat onto the dirt floor.

I get an immense amount of satisfaction.

For years he abused me. It may not have been with his fists, but it was just as dangerous.

It almost killed me.

Though I'd like to witness Roy get some more just desserts, I shift on my feet to the true culprit of the latest crime wave to hit Vegas.

I was already slotting the pieces of the puzzle together, but the picture became clear when I attended a meeting with Nero in Nikolai's office.

When I look at Tasha as if it is the first time we've met, I don't see her svelte frame that would have been revolted at the thought of eating greasy burgers and fries to make it through the week alive, or the glossiness of her hair that couldn't look bad no matter how disastrous the hair day.

I look at the woman behind decades of perceptions and years of false idolizations.

That's when I truly see her, and the dilation of her pupils when I smile announces she is aware her cloak has been stolen.

As I raise my hand to Tasha's mouth to remove her gag, Nero issues her a stern warning. "If your teeth get anywhere near her fingers, I will saw your hands off and feed them to you."

His threat shouldn't turn me on, but it does. Confidence doesn't solely come from within. It comes with the utmost certainty that someone will be there to catch you anytime you may fall.

Nero is that man for me.

The way he defended me to Nikolai assures me of this, not to mention how he's letting me take the lead in our latest coup.

I remove Tasha's gag without incident before shifting my focus to the pain in her eyes.

"It hurts, doesn't it?" Confusion blasts through her eyes, forcing me to clarify. "Not being seen."

She scoffs at me. "Please. I was so seen *your* husband couldn't get enough."

Her snippy attitude doesn't dint my confidence in the slightest because I wasn't referring to Roy. I was talking about how even being the prettiest, shiniest object in a room of despair can't force Nero's eyes to rake her body once.

Although grubby, her clothing is risqué and she has a ton of cleavage on display, yet Nero isn't the least bit interested.

I'll keep Roy's horndog expression to myself. I don't want to make you sick.

"Was it like that the first time?"

Nero warns Tasha to watch her fucking tone when she snaps out, "First time what? You're acting as if you know me."

"I do know you," I bite back, giving her a small snippet of the attention she's being denied from Nero. "You're the woman he never saw. The one who stood right in front of him, dying for an ounce of his attention, but was not awarded a single snippet of it. You may as well have been invisible because he was *never* going to look at you how you looked at him."

I twist to face Nero, who appears as lost as Roy. He is an amazing actor. "When I met your mother on the first day of the rebuild, the entire crew was here. Contractors, electricians, plumbers, and an interior designer team who had allegedly cut off their noses to spite their faces by offering their services for well below market value."

I return my eyes to Tasha in enough time to watch her throat work hard to swallow.

The quote I found in Nero's room matched the details of the business my assets had been transferred to.

It is then that Tasha's ruse started unraveling.

"There was so much buzz that day, but hardly any of it centered around the build. Everyone, including yourself, was excited about the owner's anticipated arrival later that afternoon." She lunges forward like a lunatic in a straitjacket when I mockingly whisper, "But despite killing your livelihood to get close to him, he didn't look your way once, did he?"

"He almost saw me. He was about to look straight at me!" she barks in my face, covering my cheeks with spit. "Then he saw you." She is already blistering with anger, but her next confession surges it to a pliable level. "He canceled an entire rebuild and stole months of income from his construction crew so he could watch *you* through shutters incapable of revealing how horrifying you truly are."

She spits in my face, but before Nero can pounce, I retaliate with the same level of violence.

I slap her hard across the face, sending her ranting shrieks to pained sobs.

My whack does little to weaken her campaign to slice down my confidence, but since it sees her walking straight into my trap, I don't protest. "It is disgusting. You couldn't even keep your husband's attention—"

"So you stole it before plotting ways to get back at me for

stealing Nero's devotion you wrongly believe you deserve." Everyone is stunned into silence, leaving the floor to me. "Roy wouldn't leave me, because in his own sick, twisted way, he loved me." Roy murmurs in agreement, and it makes me want to barf. "But you couldn't comprehend Nero's devotion. You've been told time and time again that beauty is rated on a clothing size, so you could never admit that he didn't want you because you are nothing close to his type."

I drag my eyes down her rake-thin frame, suddenly envious of my chunky thighs, wide hips, and squishy stomach. They gave me Nero. How could I ever hate them?

"So you hatched a plan to seduce my husband and destroy my life for warping Nero's perception of beauty." I ignore Roy's mumbled promise that she means nothing to him. "Your plan was working, but it hit a snag when Nero witnessed Roy switching my birth control tablets with placebos."

"Placebos? You said they were weight loss tablets—"

Nero slaps Roy like I did Tasha, but he uses the back of his hand and a heap more force. "Last warning, fuckface. Say another bad word about her, or insinuate she isn't perfect how she is, and I'll pull your intestines out of your nose."

With the situation under control—because Roy is too scared by the sheer honesty in Nero's tone—I shift my focus back to Tasha.

"You must have thought you had hit the jackpot when you found Nero strung out and drunk. You had a man willing to watch a woman from afar for a year without touching her solely to uphold the sanctity of marriage, so surely he'd give even a quickie Vegas wedding everything he had to make it work." For some stupid reason, I feel sorry for her during my next sentence. "But then he requested an annulment, and your world came tumbling down."

I wait for her sob to stop rolling in the back of her throat, silently asphyxiating her, before continuing. "That's when you shifted your focus back to Roy, right? You were hopeful Nero's disdain for adulterers would end badly for him."

I twist to face Roy, amused by the fear in his eyes.

He isn't scared of Nero.

He's terrified of the confidence spanning my wings.

"When Nero killed you, and don't mistake me when I say that is precisely what he would have done if I hadn't arrived at the hotel"—Nero does not interrupt since every word I speak is gospel—"*she* would have gotten everything. My business, your 401K, *our* house. *My* dog. It was all in her name because she sucked your dick so hard that your brain no longer worked."

I'm not upset. I am disgusted at the lengths people will go to get something they haven't earned.

"And then she could have taken Nero to the cleaners, either by being a witness to your murder or by bringing the judge proof that he had allegedly 'cheated,' in the means of a positive pregnancy test since you knew the instant you yanked Roy out of my hair, Nero would have no reason to hold back his desires for a second longer." I air-quote *cheated*, faultlessly devoted to my stance that nothing Nero and I did warrants a cheaters tag.

Nero didn't stalk me once the six days he tried to give his marriage a go.

Well, not in person, anyway.

Online surveillance doesn't count.

I return my eyes to Tasha. "Since neither of those options are now available, you're left with two new choices." She looks bored, so it is only fair I make things more interesting for her. "Either sign the annulment paperwork and transfer the titles of the items you stole back to me, or I'll let Nero kill you as he pleaded to do only an hour ago."

She glares at me like I don't have it in me.

She doesn't know me at all.

I'm sick of being shit on, and it is time to take a stance.

Will that include murder? I'm highly doubtful, but you don't realize how strong you are until someone pushes so hard that you are forced to shove back.

"I—"

"Option one or two. They are the only words I permit to leave your mouth."

I can't see Nero, but I know he is hard. His cock forever thickens when my confidence soars, and my panties are sticky.

"One," Tasha mumbles after a short stint of silence.

"Sorry, what was that?"

Her snivels louden along with her words. "I said number one. I take option one."

I hit her with a mocking glare. "I figured that would be the route you'd take." I turn to face Roy. "I don't want everything like she did. I just want what is rightfully mine."

"You can have it," he mumbles, his words muffled by an annoying whine. "But—"

"Nah," Nero interrupts. "You don't have any say in these negotiations. She's going to tell you what she wants, and you're going to give them to her as you should have done the past fourteen years. Do I make myself clear?"

Roy's Adam's apple bobs up and down before his head follows. "Yes."

Nero looks disappointed. He has a bone to pick, and Roy's scrawny legs are far too skinny to make a meal from. "Good."

After butting his gun at Tasha's temple, Nero releases her from her restraints so she can sign the paperwork we had pushed through in a hurry.

Her signature is messy but close to the one on her driver's license.

Roy's is far messier.

It demands a stern threat. "If you try to make out these documents are fraudulent, I'll let Nero bring you back here, but I'll ask him to place the feet of his chair on your crotch instead of your toes."

His next two signatures are easily readable. They match the one on the marriage certificate I plan to shred the instant these forms are processed through the courts.

After pulling me behind him to shelter me from any more harm from these two lunatics, Nero gives them their marching orders. They scramble for the exits, their movements remarkably fast considering the circumstances of their detainment.

Once Tempy's barks alert us to unwanted guests in the street and her dislike of Roy, Nero turns to face me.

I smile like my insides aren't twisted up in knots when he says, "Now *our* second game of chase can begin." He drags me forward before brushing his mouth over my kiss-stung lips. "This one will be nowhere near as fun as our first foray but just as rewarding."

20

NERO

"Anything yet?"

Nikolai cusses like a fifteen million wholesale loss isn't a drop in the ocean compared to what he has in offshore accounts when I shake my head. I understand why. The investigation into the missing coke isn't about the money. It is the respect he's endeavoring to return to the Popov name, and the stigma that he isn't a man you should mess with.

"And not from a lack of surveillance. Roy and Tasha haven't left our sight for a single second. If they know where the goods are, they're keeping its location under wraps."

Miranda helped me convince Nikolai that she was not a part of the sting that stole the equivalent of fifty million in street value from him by using the same investigative skills that's kept me out of trouble the past twenty-five years.

She's trusting her gut.

"I think we need to cast the net further. It is someone close to us, but maybe they're not as close as I once believed."

I hate the words the instant they leave my mouth. My gut got me to where I am, but I can't continue waiting for Tasha or Roy to make their move.

The more time I spend on them, the less time I have with Miranda.

I haven't touched her in days, and it is fucking killing me.

"Or perhaps we should bring them back and force them to speak."

Nikolai doesn't seem opposed to the idea. His curiosity and impending nuptials are the only things keeping his head in this game.

"You still think it's them?"

I half shrug, half nod. I'm the most indecisive I've ever been.

There's only one thing I am certain about.

"It wasn't Miranda. That is the only thread of certainty I have."

Nikolai mutters something under his breath about me being snowed under before he sits on the chair behind his big desk and pulls a cigarette out of a pack.

While lighting it, he speaks around the plumes of smoke its lighting inspires. "My *ahren* believes the same. She thinks you've got yourself a good woman. But..."

I could kill him for the delay.

"She knows how far a good woman will go to protect the man she loves." I'm lost as to where he's going with this. Thankfully, Nikolai isn't a man to tiptoe around anything. "Could Miranda

SHANDI BOYES

have stolen the coke to force you to face the truth on what you truly want?"

I *pfft. And here I was thinking I did a good job at hiding my infatuation with my neighbor.*

When Nikolai arches a brow, demanding a verbal reply, I say, "No—"

"Her wholesaler collects goods from the same docks we use to ship stock to the Yurys. She's done the run with him previously. She's smart as fuck. It wouldn't take much for her to put two and two together."

His attempt to soothe my matchhead short temper with compliments is pointless. "She didn't do this. She wouldn't." I ball my hands, fighting like fuck not to turn our worded exchange into a physical one. "She would tack her husband's dissected balls to the wall for me, but she wouldn't..." My words trail off when I recall the last time I mentioned someone's nuts being tacked to a wall.

"What is it?" Nikolai asks, well versed on my lost-in-thought expression.

We've been working together for years. It was more pickpocketing than a billion-dollar drug trade when we were pre-teens, but you get to know people's quirks relatively fast when they've got enough intel on you to put you away for life.

I try to work through my confusion with words instead of violence. "Is Ma still doing the alterations for Justine's dress?"

Nikolai looks at me as if I've grown a second head before he jerks up his chin, mindful I wouldn't have asked if it weren't important.

"She came by earlier this week." Nothing but worship flares

176

through his eyes when he says, "Justine's stomach is growing more ravishing every day. We'll have to make a handful more adjustments before Saturday afternoon." He speaks as if Saturday isn't tomorrow.

While his eyes stray to the wall of his office, I take a moment to deliberate. I became a part of the bratva because my mother was the head tailor for Nikolai's father. She made all of Vladimir's suits from scratch, and although that man rarely respected women, he appreciated my mother's skills enough to introduce her to his number-one foot soldier.

That man was my father.

Now, my mother wouldn't piss on my father if he were on fire.

Back then, she was instantly infatuated.

She went home with him the night they met, married him the following week, and was pregnant with me in less than a month.

They had three blissful years until one of my mother's clients asked if she was nannying for her husband's wife. She laughed off her claim, finding it hilarious that she would "nanny" her own child.

Her laughter turned to tears when the woman told her about my father's other wives and children.

My mother removed us from my father's life as quickly as he entered hers, and she's not spoken a word about him or to him ever since—neither good nor bad.

I only know their story because respecting the sanctity of a marriage, and the possible outcome she would force me to face for ignoring it, was drilled into me from a young age.

I was so fearful of fucking up when I was a kid that I swore to remain celibate and to never marry.

The first pledge only lasted as long as it took for the females in my grade and those above it to grow boobs, but the last one stuck.

It only shifted when I spotted Miranda for the first time.

If I hadn't noticed the plain, boring ring on her finger too bland for a woman of her caliber, we would have celebrated our first wedding anniversary last week.

My confession makes me panicked I am more like my father than I care to admit, but my obsession with Miranda ensures I will never betray her like my father did my mother.

I never had sex without a condom before Miranda, and even with no holes evident upon its removal, I aways made my hookups take Plan B the following morning.

I think that was the start of the end for Tasha and me. I had no recollection of our union, and no evidence we had consummated said vows, but I straight up told her she either take the morning-after pill or move her shit out of my penthouse.

She took it, begrudgingly, but I saw the hate in her eyes every time she looked at me. She acted as if I'd stolen her dreams out from beneath her when, in reality, that is what she had done to me.

I hadn't touched a woman since the day my eyes landed on Miranda, and although I had no memories of my hookup with Tasha, I felt dirty. Like I had cheated.

It honestly made me feel ill—as I'm certain it would my mother if she hadn't learned the story of my supposed "affair" in the right manner.

After working my mother's many lectures and warnings

through my head, I raise my eyes to Nikolai. He's watching me, his gawk a mix of attention and unease.

His smirk turns malicious when I say, "Promise me if I bring back the coke untouched, you won't prosecute the person who took it."

"I thought you said it wasn't her."

"It wasn't."

He watches me for a handful of seconds, silently reading me, before he asks, "But you think you know who it is?"

It kills me, but I jerk up my chin.

The coke was stolen from Clark's. Only those privileged know of its whereabouts. That's why I took Miranda there. I wanted her to know this isn't just a rebound thing for me, and if she's willing to look past the stigma of my life, I'm just as willing to pretend she isn't too good for me.

Nikolai leans forward, balancing his elbows on his desk. "Is she close to you as believed?"

Again, I nod. "That's why I need your word." When he doesn't look close to agreeing to my terms, I say, "I'll bring back the coke and pay the loss of revenue for it not being distributed over the past six days."

"I don't give a fuck about the money. It is the respect—"

"That's also what this is about," I interrupt, talking fast. "The sanctity of marriage and the consequences when you break your vows."

It takes Nikolai not even a second to click to the cause of my panic. "Your ma."

He isn't asking a question, but I nod as if he is.

His eyes bounce between mine as he asks, "Why would she throw Miranda under the bus like this?"

"Because to her, Miranda is the one at fault here." I wet my lips before delivering a confession I'd planned to take to the ground. "For decades, she has blamed herself for my father's betrayal. She said if she had asked the right questions, he wouldn't have strayed."

Nikolai looks lost. I understand. I've kept quiet about my family's dramas because it isn't my burden to share.

"My father was married when he met my mother. She was wife number three."

"So?" Nikolai murmurs, still confused. "Having more than one wife is the norm in the bratva." Suddenly, his cheeks whiten. "Just don't tell my *ahren* that."

His hand itches to trek his knife across my throat when a singsong voice asks, "Don't tell me what?"

Justine waddles into his office.

No, you didn't hear me wrong. Her stomach is the size of a beach ball.

"Hey, Nero," she greets before she accepts the chair Nikolai is offering her. It doesn't have legs like the ones Nikolai and I are seated on—unless you include the one about to rise to attention when Nikolai buries his nose into her neck and breathes in deeply. "What aren't you allowed to tell me?"

Nikolai doesn't bother lying. You lose interest in being deceitful when you're strung out on a drug stronger than any on the market.

"That having more than one wife is the norm in the bratva." He pops his head up and stares straight into her eyes. "Something you'll never have to worry about. I have enough troubles keeping up with the needs of your insatiable cunt, *Ahren*. I don't want or need more."

Justine mutters something about him being crude before she flicks her eyes to me. There isn't an ounce of worry in them, proving she believes she is more than enough for Nikolai.

How do I know this? It is the same gleam Miranda's eyes got when I told Nikolai I'd walk from the millions he's lining my pockets with before I would ever place Miranda in the firing line for a crime she didn't commit.

"Why are you discussing sister wives? Is that something you're considering?"

I gag. "No. I refuse to share Miranda. Point blank. I don't care if it is with a woman or a man. She is mine and no one else's."

Justine's cheeks inflame over the rant I should have stopped after the first word.

Nikolai looks like he wants to be sick. He faces no issues pushing through the clump of vomit in his throat, though.

"Nero thinks his mother stole our missing coke."

"That isn't what I said."

He twists his lips. "It isn't the words you speak, Nero. It is the confirmation on your face."

The nonchalant way he refers to our world reveals why I was so at ease with discussing its semantics with Miranda.

If the darkness of our industry doesn't scare away the women we love, nothing will.

Justine's brows lower as her nose crinkles. "Your mother?"

When I nod, I use the sorrow on her face to my advantage.

"But Nikolai won't pardon her mistake, even if she only did it to teach me a lesson."

"Nikolai!" She glares at him like he's a naughty puppy who chewed up her favorite stiletto.

His ego feeds off every narrowed glare, but he tries to act coy. "Pardons aren't how I operate, *Ahren*."

Justine showcases some of the gall she hit the Popov crew with when she helmed the crusade to bring Nikolai home alive only months ago after he was taken by his enemies. "Then I guess it's lucky you said she stole *our* coke. That makes it as much mine as it is yours, which frees me to say"—she locks her eyes with me —"your mother won't face any prosecution from the Popov realm if the missing items are promptly returned."

"*Ahren...*" Nikolai's tone is full of silent warnings, but there's no true heat in it. He loves when his angel fans her wings as much as I love when my butterfly stretches out hers.

I know this, and so does Justine.

She peers at her husband-to-be with a sultry grin stretched across her face before she says, "Now that wasn't so hard, was it?"

I don't know what her saying references, but Nikolai is more clued on. A smirk plays at his lips as a gleam I never wish to see again passes through his eyes.

I'm out of his office before his demand for privacy leaves his mouth, my strides as confident as my belief Justine has what it takes to make Nikolai abide by her pledge.

21

NERO

*M*y mother survived in the ruthlessness of the bratva because she has the gall of a woman with a heap more power, and an inability to stand down even when she's in the wrong. The way she pegs her shoe at me when I enter her condo is a sure-fire indication, not to mention the words she spits out in Russian.

She tells me I am not the son she raised, and that if I've come to ask for forgiveness, to walk straight back out, but she is nowhere near ready to speak with me yet.

I dodge a second flung object when I don't heel to her command before following the direction from where it came.

A reason for her red-hot anger confronts me first when I enter the roomy kitchen. Tasha is sitting on one of the stools nestled around the kitchen island, eating the baked goods my mother usually makes for me.

I didn't arrive to collect my weeks' worth of supplies, because

I have the world's best baker as a neighbor, and a hunger that suddenly has nothing to do with baked goods.

"What the fuck are you doing here?"

Tasha's gleam ripens when my mother reacts negatively to my scorn.

Her aim is precise this time, and it thrusts me back three spots.

Who knew a rolling pin could be used as a deadly weapon?

"That is no way to speak to your wife. I raised you better than that."

I narrow my eyes at Tasha, warning her our discussion is far from over, before shifting my focus to my mother. "You also taught me not to steal. That if I want something, I have to earn it."

I bounce my eyes between a pair nowhere near as aged as they should be. She had me young—young enough for only the faintest wrinkles to crease the corners of her eyes.

"Where were those morals when you stole fifteen million dollars' of uncut coke from the Popovs?"

Tasha draws in a sharp breath, wordlessly announcing she had no clue my mother's theft was so significant, and the consequences such an action could invoke, before she adds words to her reply. "I had no idea she would take that much. I swear to God."

I don't trust her as far as I can throw her, which would evict her from my mother's condo with only one toss, and the distrust is heard in my tone when I point to the chair she vacated in a hurry and say, "Sit the fuck down."

"Nero!" my mother scolds at the same time Tasha says, "I swear, baby. I had no idea. I just asked her to take a little to force you back to our marital bed. I wanted you home, with me, where you promised you would forever be during our vows."

She releases a bunch of crocodile tears that instantly unearths the entirety of her ruse. My mother canoodles her as if she is her child, while promising her she hasn't done anything wrong.

"What did you tell her?"

"Enough, Nero," my mother pleads. "Your wife is upset. Can you not see that?"

"She isn't my wife. Can you not see that?" I've never snapped at my mother like this, but I'm at the end of my rope, struggling to hold on. "Is she *anything* like I would usually go for? She's blonde. I favor brunettes. She cuts people down with insults. I prefer women who lead with kindness." I drag my eyes down Tasha's body like I did the morning I woke to her standing over my bed, showing me our marriage certificate. "I like my women with meat on their bones."

"Meat? *Please,*" Tasha pushes out with a mocking laugh. "She's fat, Nero. There's a big difference between a piece of steak and a flabby slab of pork belly from a pig incapable of rationing its daily food intake."

She just made a fatal mistake. My mother is a curvy woman, has been her entire life. She's lived with the stigma of what that means for as long as she has the scars of a scorned woman.

Tasha's concern picks up when my mother moves to my side of the kitchen to gather the rolling pin she lost when she flung it at my head.

"I'm not saying all women are like that. We're built differently by God." She went too far to try to pull the good Christian girl routine on my mother, but she keeps trying. "And that's what makes us unique. It is just... *her.* Miranda is—"

"Miranda?" my mother asks, her brows as quirked as her pitch.

When Tasha remains quiet, my mother strays her dark eyes to me. A smirk plays at my lips from the hope in her eyes before I notch up my chin.

She looks pleased for me... until she remembers one factor my father's betrayal will never allow her to overlook. "But she's married, Nero. She was not yours to touch."

"She *was* married," I correct. "But that was all said and done with when she walked in on her husband with his *mistress.*"

The narrowing of my eyes and the heat of my scorn when I stare at Tasha at the end of my reply tells my mother everything she needs to know.

"You cheated on *my* son?"

Tasha's reply comes out at a million miles an hour. "He had already filed for an annulment—"

"You cheated on *my* son!" This one is more a confirmation than a question. "Get out of my house. Now!"

A broom isn't as painful to the head as a rolling pin, but it is the perfect instrument to remove rodents from your home. It and a handful of expletives in Russian deposit Tasha and her conniving ass onto the porch of my mother's condo in under thirty seconds.

"Nero, baby, please—"

Her reply is gobbled up by the brutal slam of my mother's front door.

While sucking in big breaths, my mother keeps her back facing me for several long minutes.

Fifteen years ago, I would have bolted from her expression alone when she eventually spins around. This time, I keep my feet rooted. I'm not going to lie. It is a fucking hard feat. My mother is a ballbuster. She had to be to remain on the Popovs payroll for so long. Not even some of its founders have lasted as long as she has.

"Speak. *Now.*"

It dawns on me that some of the confidence flourishing in Miranda pollenated with me as well when I say, "I will... after you're done spilling the secrets I see in your eyes."

22

MIRANDA

"*W*ait, wait, wait." A server freezes partway out of the catering tent before pivoting to face me. I wipe up the juice of a medium-cooked angus steak from the edge of a gold-rimmed plate before twisting to face my crew. "Please ensure all the plates go out spotlessly clean. They should only be smeared while being licked clean. Presentation is as important as taste."

Justine and Nikolai's wedding reception is going off without a hitch. The vows were as beautiful as the blushing bride, and the guests enjoyed the menu selection so much some have asked for a second helping of the main meal.

It is the event of all events, and I'm incredibly proud to have pulled it off after such a tumultuous week.

"How are the desserts coming?"

"Almost ready to serve," answers Shiloh, the dessert station her specialty.

She loves baking as much as I do, but she gives bland desserts a touch of sophistication with a Shiloh-inspired twist.

"Once the final plates are collected, serve the bride and groom first before moving on to their bridal party."

The lead waiter nods before peeking into the reception venue.

Millions of twinkling lights light up the naturally beautiful Vegas sky, and although it should be chilly considering we're only two weeks out from Christmas, there are so many sparks firing between the guests that I was worried the food would be overcooked by the time my staff served it.

I feel a sense of accomplishment when the desserts start being served. It signals my hectic night will soon come to an end, and it brings me that much closer to seeing Nero again.

I've been so run off my feet that I haven't seen Nero since he donned the tuxedo Nikolai demanded all his groomsmen wear.

That was a painfully long seven hours ago.

Days ago, I would have overanalyzed his lengthy absence as a bad thing.

Now I see it more as delayed gratification.

That's how much confidence his attention has awarded me. I'm learning my worth and refusing to settle for second best.

My newfound faith in myself is why I've made the decision for Nikolai and Justine's wedding to be the last event I cater. I love working for myself and seeing my financial goals thrive from a strong work ethic and dedication, but catering isn't my first love.

I haven't made plans on what I should do next. I'm going to take a few weeks' leave, then put my thinking cap on.

Fingers crossed a majority of that thinking time will be done while naked in bed and sexually exhausted. That's where all my best ideas have come from of late.

"Where are the gold flakes for the Bloomsbury cupcakes?" Shiloh asks, her tone high with panic, dragging me from my naughty thoughts.

She's been sweating all afternoon, striving to ensure she delivers the perfect dessert platter for Justine and Nikolai's guests. Anyone would swear she has already accepted my offer for her to take over the ownership of my catering company.

I take a moment to deliberate before the light finally switches on.

"I left them in the catering van."

My head was a mess this afternoon when I was packing the goods from Clark's to have them delivered to the Popov mansion. Nikolai's crew was on hand to assist, but when news broke that I had used some of his stolen cocaine to bake away my depression, the mood sobered.

I, along with numerous members of the Popov crew, thought my head would be on the chopping block.

Mercifully, it wasn't.

The street value of the flour in my pantry was higher than the wholesale price of the goods Nero's mother had stolen, and the deficit was made up by selling the goods I had made.

Consuming cocaine is far more dangerous than snorting it or smoking it in a pipe, but its stimulation is more direct to the brain from ingestion, so it has become some users' method of choice.

Wrapping it in sugary treats is an avenue Nikolai's crew had never considered, but I see it being on the agenda at future meetings with how fast the goods Nero didn't consume sold.

It is fortunate Nero's sweet tooth had him veering for the slices and treats that were gluten free, or my baking efforts that afternoon could have killed him as Roy falsely claimed my sweet tooth would kill me—it would have just been decades faster.

When Shiloh stares at me with wide eyes and a sweat-dotted brow, I say, "I'll go grab them."

She mouths her thanks before she returns to curling the chocolate ribbons that will sit behind cupcakes and gold-dipped chocolate strawberries.

"Sorry," I apologize when I bump into someone partway to my van.

It's parked close enough to the catering tent to be walkable, but far enough away not to distract from the natural beauty of Nikolai's chosen location to marry his *ahren*.

My steps slow when the voice of the person I bumped into registers as familiar. "Why are you in such a hurry, Mir? Did you finally realize you're too good for these men?"

As I twist to face Roy, my panic surges. I'm not worried about me. I don't want his arrival pulling Nero away from the wedding reception of one of his closest friends.

"What are you doing here, Roy?"

He steps closer, filling the air and my senses with his boozy breath. "I want to speak with you."

"Then you should have picked a better location and time. I don't have time to talk to you right now. I'm busy."

I commence walking again, only to be stopped by a snivel. "I've tried to see you since... since..."

"Since you were forced to face the consequences of *your* actions?"

He nods, darkening his eyes further when the cap hiding the perfect word for his betrayal lowers down his forehead. "But *he* wouldn't give me the chance. He told me if he saw me anywhere near you, he'd kill me." The way he sneers "he" announces who he is speaking about, but before I can warn him I won't be held accountable for my actions if he mocks Nero in front of me again, he continues. "I made a mistake—"

"A mistake?" I "ha!" him. "It was more than once, and I'm not solely talking about the pictures that surrounded your feet in the hotel room you booked for your mistress."

I'm not asking a question, but he acts as if I am. "They meant nothing to me."

I scoff before I continue for the van.

He follows me like a lost dog, but I don't feel an ounce of sympathy that he may end up alone and on the streets.

My empathy commenced disappearing the day he called me a heffer for the first time, and it fully vanished when he referred to Nero as *he*.

"Stop following me, Roy," I warn when I hear footsteps. "Because I make no promises that my van is knife-free."

"Stop this, Mir. You're not like them." He thrusts his hand at the reception area whose noise subdues a smidge when his shouts reach some guests' ears. "So why the fuck are you acting like violence is the solution for everything?"

"How do you know I'm not like them?" I ask, my tone lower than his, but my anger way higher. "Even after fourteen years, you don't know a damn thing about me. Not a single thing."

"I know that I love you and that you love me. You're just

blinded by the shiny new toy *pretending* he likes you how you are now."

His eyes lower down my body.

They don't spark with envy.

He looks disgusted.

"I give him days before he either loses interest in you or puts you on a diet."

I laugh. It is witchlike and full of disbelief. "Nero is *nothing* like you." I don't wait for him to bite at the bait I'm dangling in front of him. I hit him with the utmost truths. "And that love you're talking about isn't close to what true love feels like. I *thought* I loved you, but I am learning that love isn't being belittled by your other half, being badgered by them to the point you consider suicide, and it isn't being fat shamed in front of an audience with the hope it will double the loss on the scales the following week. It isn't breaking someone's soul and then walking away without offering to pick up the pieces *you* smashed. That isn't love, Roy. That's abuse."

"Mir—"

"No. You don't deserve my time." I spin before a fire inside me forces me to spin right back around. "You also don't deserve me."

I work his coping mechanism like a pro when he follows my trek. I ignore him while stomping across manicured lawns, while throwing open the back door of my catering van, and while pulling out the sheets of gold-flecked paper Shiloh needs.

I don't speak a word until he pushes too hard for me not to respond. "I'm your fucking husband! That should award me some morsel of respect."

"Wrong. You *were* my husband. You're not anymore." The hairs on my nape prickle before they fortify the rod in my back. But the person inspiring them remains hidden, confident I've got this. "So get the fuck out of my life before the only title our marriage will leave me with is widower."

Roy is an idiot. I can't put it any simpler than that.

"You—"

"Nah," Nero mutters, moving out of the curtains stopping the bugs from entering the catering tent. "You don't have a say in *any* of her decisions. You shouldn't have had any back then, and I sure as fuck won't let you have any now."

"Jesus, Mir... You move fast."

Roy glares at me as if I am a whore, but before Nero can pounce, I retaliate.

I wipe his sneer off his face with my fist.

Unlike Nero, Roy doesn't remain standing. He crumbles to the ground, his hand shooting up to caress his cheek.

I could stay to relish his cowardly sobs, but I have an event to host and a business to run. Furthermore, my time is too precious to waste a single second on a man who has only ever loved himself.

"Once you've finished taking out the trash, I could use a hand, if you're up to it?"

The tugging of Nero's chunky lips announces he heard my comment as intended, not to mention the gravelly deliverance of his words when he reminds me that I will always come first in his eyes. "I'll never be too busy for you, butterfly."

With two clicks of Nero's tattooed fingers, Eight arrives out of nowhere, hoists Roy off the ground, and then tosses him into the back of a blacked-out SUV as if he is a ragdoll.

Just as fast, Nero's front heats my back and his breaths flutter my ear. "You just need to tell me where you need me the most, butterfly, and for how fucking long you want me."

"Forever" is the first word out of my mouth. It is closely followed by "And everywhere."

23

NERO

Six weeks later...

*M*iranda screams my name in a mangled roar when I flip her over without removing my cock from her tight, wet cunt. Her flexibility and the bounce of her sexy thighs as they skim over my sweat-drenched chest harden me further.

I love taking her hard and fast from behind, but this... having every inch of her glorious body displayed in front of me is the stuff dreams are made of.

I love the way her tits clap when I fuck her without remorse, and the jiggles of her ass when my balls slap against them for each brutal pound.

The sex has been relentless for the past six weeks, but I still can't get enough.

Every time I have her, I become more addicted.

I'm a full-blown fucking addict.

Not even giving her the title of my wife subdued my wish to have this beautiful woman beneath me, on top of me, and covering every fucking inch of me.

Don't act surprised by how fast I moved. I wasn't lying when I said I would have given Miranda my last name the week we met if she weren't already married.

As Rico Popov would say, *"You don't wait when an angel falls into your lap. You grant her every wish."*

You also shouldn't misconstrue the strength of my butterfly. I haven't forced Miranda to do anything against her wishes. I helped crack her cocoon and fan her wings, but the freedom that comes from a weightless flight is limitless.

She was a willing participant in our Vegas quickie wedding two weeks ago where my mother and Tempy were our witnesses, and she's put as many hours into the event we will host for our family and friends in the spring to announce our marriage as Shiloh has.

My woman is as snowed under as I am, and I can't wait to tick off every item on her wish list.

There are only two wishes I've yet to fulfill.

One I'm working on now.

Two will have to wait until I've finished fucking my wife to oblivion.

Nothing comes before Miranda's pleasure.

Not a single fucking thing.

I shift the tilt of Miranda's hips, bringing them up and forward, before I add a roll to my pumps. Her eyes roll into the back of her head when the rim of my cock rubs at the sensitive spot inside her.

I strive for no color to be seen by reaching between us and rolling her clit with my thumb.

"I need you to come for me again, *printsessa*. Give my sperm clear passage to your egg like a good little wifey."

Miranda's grip of the bedding is so rigid her knuckles go white. She moans through every thrust and accepts me without protest.

She feels so good.

Tight.

Wet.

About to be carrying my kin.

We dumped her birth control the day we wed, and although Miranda said it might take a few weeks to leave her system, we've been acting as if its ineffectiveness is immediate.

I've lost count of the number of times I pushed my sperm back inside her before it gets close to smudging the pillow I stuff under her ass to heighten the chances of conception.

That's how fucking obsessed I am of the idea of her stomach being swollen with my child.

I love her curves, but wondering how they'll develop while she's growing my child... *fuck.*

I fuck her harder. *Faster.* I drive into her so ruefully the emasculating pink bed frame she bought to stick it to Roy bounces across the wooden floorboards of her bedroom.

The same word falls from my mouth with every skid.

Mine.

Mine.

Mine.

The possessiveness of my pumps and the swivels of my thumb on her clit bring Miranda's screams up to an ear-piercing level.

Beads of sweat roll off my cheeks and dot the mound of her pussy, adding to the slickness coating my shaft.

She's so close to release again that I can taste her arousal on the tip of my tongue.

"Oh..." Her back arches as her head thrusts back. "I'm... I'm..."

"Give it to me, *printsessa*. Come on my dick. Strangle it with the greedy sucks of your pussy."

Miranda stills, then moans, her expression both beautiful and destroyed.

I've lost count to the number of orgasms she's faced today, but each one is more powerful than the one before it.

Her climax lasts for an eternity and zaps the last of her energy.

She's floppy and pliable by the time she finishes shaking, exactly how I want her.

I continue pumping into her, admiring the heavy rise and fall of her chest, before I bury myself deep inside her and then grunt through a brutal release.

Her beautiful eyes snap open when my hot, salty sperm pumps inside her, filling her already brimming pussy.

Moaning, she massages my twitching shaft, milking me of every drop of cum while maintaining eye contact.

It is intimate as fuck and proves what I have always known.

She has me by both the balls and my heart.

———

"I'll forget how to use my wings if you forever carry me everywhere."

I grunt like I'm not opposed to the idea before I continue moving through her home, dodging Tempy's excited twirls and begs. We fucked on the couch downstairs because we were too impatient to climb the stairs, and then Miranda rested while my sperm hopefully worked its magic.

I wouldn't have moved her if it weren't important.

"Do you want to shower before getting dressed? Or are you happy getting around smelling like my cum?"

I'm hard enough to drill the Antarctic when the lusty gleam in her eyes answers my question on her behalf.

I set her down in front of her walk-in closet before returning to the living room to collect Tempy. The deck outside catches as much sun as the one on the second-floor balcony, but the sun is dropping quicker now that Christmas has passed.

It's colder than a witch's tit—another strong point as to why I needed to wake Miranda.

"Where are we going, again?" Miranda asks from inside her closet, aware of my return from Tempy whining when I place her down. She's as obsessed with licking my face as I am of licking her owner's delicious pussy.

When I growl, Miranda pops her head out of the closet. "I was just asking so I can coordinate the perfect outfit. I don't want to look frumpy." Her last sentence is a whisper, but not even a tornado siren could have me missing it.

"What the fuck did you just say?"

She'd usually reevaluate her words when it puts me on the warpath to restore the confidence a worthless prick stole from her, but this time, she repeats them. "I don't want to look frumpy."

As I join her in the closet, I run the short list of people she interacted with today through my head. I don't care that they're a member of Nikolai's crew. I'll kill them without a second thought if they're responsible for her dip in confidence.

"What was the name of that punk with the buck teeth who opened the door for you today? The valet."

Miranda shrugs. "I don't know."

She's lying. I know this, and so does she.

"Acting daft won't save him from my wrath, butterfly. If he said something bad to you, he's dead."

"He didn't say anything bad."

"So he said something?"

"Yes, but it isn't what you're thinking."

I *pfft* like I don't believe her, and it makes her giggle.

I'm glad she's amused. I am about to go on a fucking rampage, and she's laughing.

What the fuck am I missing?

"He said that I was glowing."

"Flirting with *my wife* is just as bad as insulting her."

Miranda fans her hand across my chest, loving my jealousy, before she balances on her tippy-toes to brush her mouth against mine. She doesn't kiss me. She simply hammers the final nail in the valet's coffin. "Then he congratulated me. I assumed he was talking about our recent nuptials... until his eyes lowered to my stomach."

I pull away, ready and willing to kill him. Insinuating that a woman is pregnant because she's put on a couple of pounds is bullshit. Miranda has put on a little weight in the past six weeks, but that's because she is eating three solid meals a day instead of sneaking downstairs after dark to consume something other than lettuce leaves.

Roy starved her—of both affection and food.

I refuse to be anything like that prick.

"Pack a coat. It is cold in the woods where I'll bury him."

Miranda laughs as if I am joking. I'm not. My stories about the numerous unmarked graves in the woodlands between the Popov mansion and Clark's were one hundred percent factual.

"I was about to give him the serving of his life." Miranda has to shout to ensure I can hear her over my stomps, and her next words force my eyes back on the prize. "Then I realized his assessment of the situation could be on point." She nervously chews on her bottom lip while confessing, "I'm late."

It shouldn't take almost a minute to work out that two plus two equals four, but that's how long it takes for me to do the math.

We've fucked every day, multiple times a day, for the past six weeks.

She's not bled once.

"If I am pregnant, I swear to God it's yours. Roy and I—"

I stuff her worry into the back of her throat along with the remainder of her words when I storm across the room, rake my fingers through her hair, and then kiss her with everything I have.

I kiss her until the sun disappears with her worry.

I kiss her until her happiness matches mine.

And I kiss her until I wonder what the fuck I'm going to do with the little bakery I purchased three blocks over, and the millions of dollars I invested to make it everything Miranda dreamed of when she was a child with a record-breaking rebuild schedule.

EPILOGUE
MIRANDA

Four and a half years later...

"*W*ait, wait, wait. They need their toppers." I scan a long counter covered with flour, seeking the graduation caps I made earlier this week. "They have to be here somewhere."

I squeal in excitement when I find them under a stack of paperwork I made Shiloh promise to leave in my capable hands during her long-awaited leave.

After bundling them into a container that will assist in maintaining their shape, I place them on top of the cupcakes Shiloh is precariously balancing, then guide her out of a stuffy yet delicious-smelling kitchen.

"The graduation caps are super cute, but I bet they were a fucker to make."

Incapable of arguing, I blow a wayward hair out of my face

before slipping into the driver's seat of the catering van, forgetting I'm no longer the lead driver or head honcho of this business.

"Sorry. Old habits die hard."

"Clearly." Shiloh laughs. "It's only been four and a half years."

After playfully bumping her with my hip, I remove the carton of cupcakes from her arms and then switch positions.

I slot into the passenger seat as Shiloh slips behind the steering wheel.

Well, as well as she can with her rapidly expanding stomach.

She's so close to her due date her stomach is almost touching the steering wheel. She's glowing, and it has my thoughts shifting back to the day I was complimented about the same glow.

God, that feels like a lifetime ago. My life has changed so much since then. It honestly feels like decades have passed.

"Are you sure you want to do this?" Shiloh asks upon spotting my white cheeks.

Peering at my heart-shaped face in the side mirror, I pinch some color into my cheeks before jerking up my chin. "As ready as I'll ever be."

She squeezes my hand in support before she turns down a familiar street. My stomach does somersaults when she parks in a driveway across the street from the house I once shared with Roy.

I haven't stepped foot in it in over three years, but I can still recall the floor space with ease.

"I'll get her," I say when Shiloh unlatches her belt and curls her hand around the door latch.

Her eyes are on me, misty and uneased. "Are you sure? I don't mind. I don't want things to get... *awkward*."

"I'm sure."

I'm not, but what else can I say in a situation like this? Shiloh is my best friend, but some things you need to keep to yourself.

"I'll be right back."

I straighten my coat before walking briskly down the paved path. The doorbell barely rings before it is yanked open so forcefully that it almost comes off its hinges.

"Mommy!"

Bella leaps into my arms and hugs me like she hasn't seen me in weeks before she peers up at me with big, hungry eyes.

I'm a sucker for her begging stare.

"The cupcakes are in the car with Shiloh. I packed an extra one just for you."

"Thank you, Mommy!" she shouts before she pivots on her heels to gather her backpack from her father, and her graduation outfit she won't need until this afternoon, before she bolts past me.

I try to act like my heart isn't pattering in my ears when her father joins me in the foyer. He smells divine, his scent unchanging even with him going through fatherhood. It is as dark and dangerous as ever, and it sets my pulse racing.

"Hey, butterfly," Nero greets as his eyes rake my body. "You look pretty."

"This?" I wave off his compliment as if it is one in a trillion I receive per day. "It's nothing special."

Nero appears as if he wants to say something, but the annoying honk of an impatient woman stops him.

"I should get going. I don't want Bell late for her official last day of preschool."

As awkwardly as I did the first time I left his presence, I wave like a fool, then follow the steps our daughter recently took.

Shiloh eyeballs me while reversing out of the driveway of Nero's first off-compound purchase. Her stare is full of suspicion, and it makes me super-hot.

After a beat, she murmurs, "That went better than anticipated."

She can say that. She can't feel how sweaty I am under my coat. I'm a messy, sticky inferno.

My unease slips away when I peer back at Bella in her car seat. Her face is covered with butter icing, and her hands are as sticky as the cups of my new bra.

I've only just cleaned her up when we arrive at her school.

"Yoohoo! Miranda."

Ms. Croft, Bella's teacher, waves us to a reserved spot at the front of the drop-off line. That's how desperate she is for my baked goods. Though she does treat me like a VIP every time I do a school visit, so perhaps it has nothing to do with the cupcakes I promised her class.

I'm pulled from my thoughts when Ms. Croft says, "Oh, Miranda. You've outdone yourself. These cupcakes are fantastic."

"Thank you," I reply, genuinely flushed from the sheer delight in her tone.

Needing to leave before the heat roaring through my body forces me to unbutton my coat, I kiss Bella goodbye before slipping into Shiloh's van and demanding she floor the gas.

We're barely two blocks away when I'm reminded daftness isn't solely reserved for fresh-out-of-college women.

"I forgot the candle for the cake."

Shiloh shrugs. "So?"

"It's a birthday cake. You can't have a birthday cake without a candle." I take a moment to deliberate before saying, "Go to my house. It will be quicker than detouring back to the bakery."

"Do you want me to call ahead and see if the hotel has a candle you can borrow? We're already behind."

I shake my head. "Just go back to my house."

She huffs before giving in.

"I'm sorry," she screams at the person she cuts off when she conducts a dangerous U-turn.

Shiloh's lead foot sees us arriving home in under a minute, and I race down the footpath just as fast.

While Tempy dances around my feet, I check my baking stock in the massive walk-in pantry, and the junk drawer every American has in their kitchen, before I search for a candle in the cupboards above the refrigerator.

I find what I'm seeking just as a deep, delicious voice asks, "Don't you think it is a little warm for a coat, butterfly?"

I swallow the lump in my throat before carefully stepping off the stepladder and turning to face the voice. "Nero, what are you doing here?"

He steps closer, unshadowing his devastatingly handsome face and forcing my thighs to touch. "This is my house."

His dark and dangerous eyes lower to the daring flap of my trench coat for half a second before they slowly return to my face.

They're brimming with lust and are very much possessive.

"And you are my wife. Where else am I meant to be?"

My confusion gets a moment of reprieve when I stray my eyes to the kitchen counter. The note I left there this morning appears untouched. Does that mean he's clueless that I cleared his schedule so he could meet me at his latest hotel for brunch?

There's nothing of sustenance on the menu I planned for him —except my husband's most craved palette. Me!

"Did you not eat breakfast this morning?" I ask, my tone as stern as Nero is anytime Bella tries to skip a meal so she will remain as skinny as her favorite pop stars. I left my note next to his favorite mug. It was his Father's Day present last year, and it showcases his three most valued things.

Images of me, Bella, and our unborn son.

"I ate." I'm on the cusp of combustion when Nero licks his lips before he murmurs, "Twice." His expression is a mix of emotions. I learn why when he says, "The second meal I was supplied wasn't edible. Bell didn't inherit her mother's cooking skills. Let's pray they can be taught."

When he moves closer, incapable of not responding when he makes me smile, I fan my hand across his chest. "Stay back. You'll ruin the surprise if you come any closer."

"If it is *my* surprise, it is *mine* to ruin." He couldn't sound more possessive if he tried. "So get your fine ass over here now, *printsessa*, and feed your man. I'm fucking starved."

It's been like this our entire marriage. We can't keep our hands off each other when we're in the same vicinity. That's why I went to the bakery Nero purchased me as a wedding gift to get ready for his surprise. He'd kick down the bathroom door if denied the opportunity of touching me for even a minute while we're under the same roof.

The number-one bakery in Vegas wasn't the ideal location to prepare his ultimate birthday treat, but since my baby brain had me forgetting the cupcakes I promised Bella's classmates, it worked out well.

Nero is never suspicious of my early-morning starts at our now multiple bakery sites, because for the eight months of my first pregnancy, he was right there with me, making sure I didn't lift a finger, while excessively doting on me.

Our joint business endeavor should have flopped weeks in. Fortunately for us, treats inspired by love are extremely profitable.

We're in the process of expanding our franchise across the country.

Air hisses between Nero's teeth when he tugs open the coat hiding his birthday present. I'm around the same size I was when we met, but my stomach is puffed out with our son, who is due in a little over four months, making Nero even more obsessed with my curves.

My lingerie leaves nothing to the imagination, and since it is edible and molded around my breasts to look like birthday cakes, it makes me incredibly grateful Bella struggled to make her father a bowl of cereal for his fortieth birthday.

Nero's eyes rocket to mine when I say, "What do you say, birthday boy, bite for a bite, and lick for a lick?"

The End!

Facebook: facebook.com/authorshandi

. . .

Instagram: instagram.com/authorshandi

Email: authorshandi@gmail.com

Reader's Group: bit.ly/ShandiBookBabes

Website: authorshandi.com

Newsletter: https://www.subscribepage.com/AuthorShandi

ALSO BY SHANDI BOYES

Denotes Standalone Books

Perception Series

Saving Noah *

Fighting Jacob *

Taming Nick *

Redeeming Slater *

Saving Emily

Wrapped Up with Rise Up

Protecting Nicole *

Enigma Series

Enigma

Unraveling an Enigma

Enigma The Mystery Unmasked

Enigma: The Final Chapter

Beneath The Secrets

Beneath The Sheets

Spy Thy Neighbor *

The Opposite Effect *

I Married a Mob Boss *

Second Shot *

The Way We Are

The Way We Were

Sugar and Spice *

Lady In Waiting

Man in Queue

Couple on Hold

Enigma: The Wedding

Silent Vigilante

Hushed Guardian

Quiet Protector

Enigma: An Isaac Retelling

Twisted Lies *

Bound Series

Chains

Links

Bound

Restrain

The Misfits *

Nanny Dispute *

Russian Mob Chronicles

Nikolai: Resurrecting the Bratva

Nikolai: Resurrecting the Bratva

Nikolai: Ruling the Bratva

Asher: My Russian Revenge *

Trey *

Nero: Shattered Wings *

The Italian Cartel

Dimitri

Roxanne

Reign

Mafia Ties (Novella)

Maddox

Demi

Ox

Rocco *

Clover *

Smith *

RomCom Standalones

Just Playin' *

Ain't Happenin' *

The Drop Zone *

Very Unlikely *

False Start *

Short Stories - Newsletter Downloads

Christmas Trio *

Falling For A Stranger *

One Night Only Series

Hotshot Boss *

Hotshot Neighbor *

The Bobrov Bratva Series

Wicked Intentions *

Sinful Intentions *

Devious Intentions *

Deadly Intentions *

Martial Privilege Series

Doctored Vows *

Deceitful Vows *

Vengeful Vows *

Broken Vows *

Made in the USA
Las Vegas, NV
28 August 2025

27098235R00125